A Voyage to the Moon

A Voyage to the Moon

Cyrano de Bergerac

Translated by Andrew Brown

ALMA CLASSICS

ALMA CLASSICS
an imprint of

ALMA BOOKS LTD
3 Castle Yard
Richmond
Surrey TW10 6TF
United Kingdom
www.101pages.co.uk

A Voyage to the Moon first published in French as *L'Autre Monde, ou Les États et Empires de la Lune* in 1657
This translation first published by Hesperus Press Ltd in 2007
This edition first published by Alma Classics in 2019

Translation, Introduction and Notes © Andrew Brown, 2007, 2019

Cover design by Will Dady

Printed in Great Britain by CPI Group (UK) Ltd, Croydon CR0 4YY

ISBN: 978-1-84749-799-4

Contents

Introduction

Yes, the moon can still make you catch your breath as it hovers there, a delicate crescent, against the stars on a cold winter's night – other-worldly, enigmatic and magical – but you know that creatures of your kind have left their footprints there and even played golf on its silent, dusty surface. William Empson wrote a poem ('To an Old Lady') about the risks entailed by demystifying the moon, but the poem also accepts the inevitability of this process. The moon is a celestial marvel, but it is not immune from Max Weber's "disenchantment of the world".

Cyrano's book too is partly about the interweaving of symbolic enchantment and comical, disenchanted satire. Its real title is *The Other World*. Or rather, the full manuscript title reads: *L'Autre Monde, ou Les États et Empires de la Lune* (*The Other World, or the States and Empires of the Moon*). The title by which the work is more often known in French, *Voyage dans la Lune*, has stuck, and has a certain convenience to it, as Cyrano is in the line of the many science-fiction writers (Lucian, Verne, Wells) who have imagined a trip to the moon both for the sheer imaginative fascination of the thing, and also for political commentary and philosophical speculation. But *The Other World* is a good title, encapsulating the restless jokey dialectic of the story: the moon is earth's moon (i.e. satellite), but from another point of view the earth is the moon's moon. So we are each other's moon or Other (see the video clips, still awesome, of earth rise over the moon, taken from *Apollo 8*): the values of the one world are often the counter-values of the other. And if the moon is an Other, it too has an Other – the sun! This is also inhabited: Socrates' demon, who comes to guide the narrator, is one such solar denizen – and we are invited to speculate on the myriad other worlds extending through space. We have moved from the concentric circles of Ptolemy to the ballet of the stars in *2001*. And while "the other world" often implies transcendence (Paradise, for instance, or life after death – probably the sense of the last ironic words of Cyrano's novel), it is a transcendence that is constantly being tugged down to earth (or should that be the "moon"?...).

Cyrano's fable is truly speculative ("what if?...") rather than dogmatic: what if there were creatures on the moon who had never heard the Gospel; what if respect were paid to youth rather than age; what if our "ideas" were not just mental constructs but rather the impressions of subtler senses than those we usually acknowledge? Cyrano's text gives voice to some of the most "advanced" thinking of his time (the movement of the earth, the plurality of worlds, the possible infinite extent of the universe, the way that suns and their planets may be destroyed and reborn, heliocentrism, atheism, materialism and various other more or less beguiling isms), but always in an exploratory and extravagant way. One of Cyrano's favourite words is "tickle": our senses are tickled by matter, our minds are tickled by his fantasies. As with all tickling, this can sometimes go too far, and the reader is left gasping for breath at the torrent of absurdly counter-intuitive speculations that Cyrano unleashes. But many of his imaginings (talking books, for example) have now become everyday contrivances, and even Cyrano's most far-fetched conceits are variations on pre-existing themes that, like a musician playing with fugues and canons, he reverses or plays backwards. Thus, rather than inventing new stories, Cyrano takes fugal flights of fancy on the back of the old "canonical" ones (many taken from the Bible), and has great fun with the myths and fables he has inherited. He puts flesh on Socrates' demon and at the same time turns it into a protean spirit able to infuse itself into many different bodies. He relocates the Garden of Eden to the moon, and rewrites the story of both the Fall and (in an episode worthy of Baron Munchausen) the Flood. He deploys a vocabulary that, for the purists of the neoclassical age, might well have appeared shockingly vulgar and overfond of neologism. He merrily uses and abuses technical terms, while showing a lack of *pudeur* in the naming of parts both bodily and mechanical. He anticipates balloon flight (the Montgolfiers, no less, acclaimed him as a precursor) and invents various thought experiments that look forward to Einstein. And he generally indulges his imagination in every kind of daring speculation, as we would expect from this *libertin* (a freethinker, but also one inclined to libertinage, the pleasures of the flesh – and the mind). He would no doubt have endorsed the way the moon people take leave of each other with the words *Songez à librement vivre*, "Remember to live freely". This was not easy in the seventeenth century: his manuscript circled in samizdat among the underground intelligentsia of his day, and was published only after his death, in an expurgated version edited by a friend of his who was also a priest.

Cyrano allows his characters to voice powerful criticisms of the Church, of traditional Aristotelian physics and Ptolemaic cosmology, and of his own society's accepted values. But he also makes us wonder about the relativity of all values. Pascal was doing something similar in his *Pensées*: what is right this side of the Pyrenees is wrong on the other side – an idea of considerable antiquity (Xenophanes said that Ethiopians worshipped gods who were as snub-nosed as they themselves were). For Cyrano, what is right in this world (on earth) is often wrong on the other (the moon), and both are wrong, or at least questionable, when seen from the sun (a world he explores in the companion piece to this, *The States and Empires of the Sun*). But the relativism is not vacuous and abstract, but critical and concrete: though he adopts a bracingly non-anthropocentric view of the world in which cabbages are the equal of kings, the powers and potentials of human beings are still central, and their moral failings, however material the causes behind them, are still taken seriously. In *The States and Empires of the Sun*, the birds criticize human beings for being... inhuman.

As this example shows, the critique of accepted practices in Cyrano often takes burlesque and surrealistic forms, meant to startle us out of the way we take our own lives for granted. It is as if human life were somehow being examined from the outside, by an extraterrestrial. In this unfamiliar light, other ways of thinking and behaving become possible. In Buñuel's film *The Phantom of Liberty*, we see a group of friends sitting round a dinner table; they are not eating, but reading papers and magazines, occasionally exchanging pleasantries, commenting on the day's news. Then one of them rises, excuses himself and goes to a small room where he sits down, rubs his hands and smacks his lips at the sight of the delicious meal spread in front of him, which he proceeds to tuck into. Then it dawns on us, and we realize, if we haven't already, that the apparent "diners" were in fact sitting on toilets and the apparent toilet-visitor is a diner: Buñuel is imagining a society in which people gather together in public to defecate, and closet themselves in privacy to eat. We are shocked into reflecting on our taboos. Cyrano's moon people, a little more delicately, remove their clothes to eat, but there is no orgiastic *Grande Bouffe* here: they feed on the vapours of their meals, just as the spirits who visited Yeats could drink from the fume of the wine without needing to taste the liquid. Cyrano can startle us as much as Buñuel does. On the moon, bills are paid in poems, age obeys youth, battles are decided in somewhat unmartial ways, the phallus is something to be worn with pride, dead philosophers are cannibalized. But on the whole, Cyrano's defamiliarizations are less terroristic and more epicurean. His materialism is subtle, charming and airy. He is good at machines – those of flight and locomotion in particular – his houses can walk from place to place or hunker down in the ground. But he is better at the organic, since he loves the idea that all matter is in some way animated. The hymn in praise of cabbages is both hilarious and perfectly serious – and somewhat scary, since even vegetarians are consuming sentient creatures. There is no microcosm that is not also a macrocosm: if the orbits of the planets are like the skins of an onion, the heart of an onion is also a miniature sun.

The speculations on physics are baroque and convoluted: Cyrano's world swarms and pullulates with strange energies and efflorescences. I have tried to preserve something of the at times bewildering restlessness of these imaginings (which are often broken off before they can be made systematic) in my translation: there may be a systematic theory of the physical world lurking in Cyrano's text, but I feel that it is best seen as a transitional work, happier with metaphor and metamorphosis than with post-Galilean quantitative scientific rigour.

So this is a text that moves towards increasingly bold surmises – until the Devil suddenly pops up to restore an ironic orthodoxy. But before then we have been treated to new tales about biblical figures we thought had been done to death – and they are wonderfully entertaining stories, too: subversive examples of *aggadah*, the traditional Jewish way of using narrative to amplify and divert the Scriptures. The old and the new intertwine in a fantastic dance, spiralling off into the unknown. The sun is always the same, but the moon is always changing: that is why we speak of a "new moon", and that is why we can enjoy the successive phases and fantasias of Cyrano's at times lunatic speculations.

– Andrew Brown

A Voyage to the Moon

T HE MOON WAS FULL, the sky was cloudless and the clocks had just struck nine in the evening as we – four of my friends and I – made our way home from a house not far from Paris. The various thoughts inspired in us by the sight of that saffron globe provided us with topics for conversation as we walked. Our eyes grew misty as we gazed at that great star; one of us suggested that it was a small window in the sky through which the glory of the blessed could be glimpsed, while another then protested that it was the clothes horse on which Diana hangs Apollo's collars, and yet another exclaimed that it might well be the sun himself, who, having laid aside his rays in the evening, looked down through this hole to observe what people did on earth when he was no longer around.

"I'd happily join you in your enthusiastic speculations," I said. "But I will not dally with the witty, imaginative ideas you are deploying to tickle time and make it pass more quickly; what I think is that the moon is a world just like this one, and that our world is its moon."

The company gratified me with a great burst of laughter.

"Perhaps," I said to them, "there is a person on the moon at this very minute making fun of somebody else for maintaining that this globe of ours is a world."

But however much I insisted that Pythagoras, Epicurus, Democritus and, in our own time, Copernicus and Kepler had shared this opinion, I only succeeded in making them laugh more uproariously.

This thought, whose boldness fitted well with my temper, and was made all the more stubborn by contradiction, took root so deeply in me that, for the rest of the way, I was bursting with a thousand definitions of the moon to which I could not give birth – and, by thinking up serious reasons in support of this belief, I almost convinced myself. But listen, reader, and I will tell you of the miracle, or the accident, of which Providence or Fortune availed themselves to confirm it in my mind.

I had just returned home and, seeking rest after my walk, had hardly entered my bedroom when, on my table, I found an open book that I had not placed there. It was the works of Cardano,* and although I was not intending to read it, my eyes were irresistibly drawn to a story related by this philosopher: he writes that, studying one evening by candlelight, he saw coming in through the closed doors of his room two tall elderly men; after prolonged interrogation on his part, they told him that they lived on the moon.* And saying this, they disappeared.

I was amazed both to see that a book had put itself there of its own accord and that it had done so at just that time, and open at just that particular page; I concluded that this whole chain of events was inspired by God, who wished me to reveal to mankind that the moon is a world.

"What!" I said to myself. "I have spent all day talking about a particular subject, and a book that perhaps is the only one in the world to treat of this subject just happens to fly from my bookshelves onto my table, becoming capable of reason and opening at just the place that relates such a wonderful adventure, thereby furnishing my fantasy with food for thought and my desires with new designs!... Doubtless," I continued, "the two old men who appeared to that great philosopher must be the very same who dislodged my book and opened it at this page to spare themselves the trouble of delivering to me the same lecture they gave to Cardano."

I mused further. "But surely I will not be able to find out the truth of the matter unless I travel up to the moon?"

I immediately answered my own question. "And why not? After all, Prometheus once climbed up to heaven to steal fire."

The heat of these feverish monologues was succeeded by the hope of successfully carrying out this wonderful trip. In order to realize my plans, I locked myself away in a somewhat isolated country house where, after nursing my daydreams with different ways of travelling to the moon, this is how I reached for the sky:

I tied around myself several little bottles filled with dew, and as the sun's heat attracted them, it lifted me so high that I eventually found myself above the highest clouds. But this attraction made me rise too quickly, and instead of approaching the moon as I wished, she seemed even further away from me than when I left; so I broke several of the little bottles until I felt my weight exceeding the force of attraction and started to descend back to earth.

I had had the right idea, since I landed on earth shortly afterwards; calculating from the time I had left, it should have been midnight. However, I realized that the sun was actually at its zenith and that it was midday. You can imagine how astonished I was – so astonished, indeed, that I did not know what had caused this miracle, and was arrogant enough to imagine that God had favoured my boldness by once more nailing the sun back up in the sky to shed his light on such a noble enterprise.*

I was even more bewildered because I could not recognize the country I was in. As I thought I had ascended straight up, I also thought I must have come down at the same spot from which I had left. Bearing all my accoutrements, I made my way towards a cottage from which smoke was rising, and I was hardly a pistol-shot away when I found myself surrounded by a great number of savages. They seemed completely amazed to see me – I think I must have been the first man they had ever seen wearing bottles. And what made them even more unsure of how to interpret my outlandish appearance was the fact that, as I walked, I hardly touched the ground: they did not realize that I needed only to move my body slightly, and the heat of the noonday sun's rays would make me rise up with my dew, and if I had still had a sufficient number of bottles, I might quite possibly have been swept from their sight into the air.

I started to move towards them, but, as if their panic had changed them into birds, they immediately melted away into a nearby forest. I still managed to catch one of them: no doubt his spirit had been willing to flee away, but his legs were weak. With considerable difficulty, for I was out of breath, I asked him how far we were from Paris, for how long people in France had been going around naked, and why they had run away from me in such terror. The man to whom I was speaking was an olive-hued old fellow who immediately threw himself at my feet. Putting his hands together behind his head, he opened his mouth and closed his eyes. He carried on mumbling for a long time, but I could not make out a thing he was saying and decided that his language was the hoarse chirruping of a mute.

Some time after, I saw a company of soldiers marching up with drums beating, and observed two of them leaving the main body to come and investigate me. When they were close enough for me to make myself heard, I asked them where I was.

"You're in France," they replied. "But who the devil has got you into such a state? And how is it that we don't know you? Have the ships come in? Are you going to inform the Governor? And why have you divided your brandy out into so many bottles?"

To all their questions I retorted that the Devil had not got me into that state; the reason they didn't know me was that they could not possibly know everybody; I was unaware that the River Seine carried sea vessels; I had no information for M. de Montbazon;* and I was not laden with brandy.

"Aha!" they said, seizing my arm, "we have a real joker here! Let's take you the Governor – *he'll* certainly know who you are!"

They led me towards the rest of their company as they spoke, and I learnt from them that I was in France, and yet not in Europe, since I was in New France. I was presented to M. de Montmagny, who is the Viceroy there.* He enquired after my country, my name and my quality, and when I had satisfied him by relating how my journey had been such an agreeable success (he either believed me or pretended to believe me), he kindly had a room prepared for me in his suite of apartments. I was extremely happy to meet a man capable of lofty thoughts who showed no surprise when I told him that the earth must have turned during my elevation; having started my ascent two leagues away from Paris, I had fallen almost perpendicularly onto Canada.

That evening, as I was going to bed, he came into my room.

"I would not have come to disturb your rest," he said, "unless I had thought that someone able to travel nine hundred leagues in half a day could do so without getting tired. But can you imagine," he added, "what an entertaining quarrel about you I have just had with our Jesuit fathers? They are completely convinced that you are a magician, and the best grace you can hope for from them is to pretend you're merely an impostor. Indeed, this movement you attributed to the earth is a fine paradox; what stops me sharing your opinion is that even though you left Paris yesterday, you may have arrived in this country today without the earth having turned. The sun lifted you up by means of your bottles – may it not have brought you here, since, according to Ptolemy, Tycho Brahe and the modern philosophers, the sun moves along the same route that you attribute to the earth? And, after all, what leads you to think it at all likely that the sun is motionless, when we can see it move? And why do you think that the earth turns around its centre so rapidly, when we can feel it firm beneath us?"

"Sir," I replied, "here are the reasons that lead us to those conclusions. Firstly, it is common sense to believe that the sun has taken up its place in the centre of the universe, since all the bodies in nature need this radical fire, which dwells in the heart of the kingdom just so that it may promptly satisfy their needs and so that the cause and origin of all generation may be placed equidistant from the bodies on which it acts, just as Nature in her wisdom has placed the genitals in the middle of man, the seeds in the centre of apples and kernels in the heart of fruit, and just as the onion has a hundred skins to shelter and preserve the precious germ from which ten million other onions may draw their essence. For this apple is in itself a little universe, and its seed, warmer than the other parts, is the sun which sheds heat around itself to preserve its globe; and this germ, in this onion, is the little sun of that little world, which warms and nourishes the vegetative salt of that whole mass.

"If we accept as much, then, since the earth needs the light, the heat and the influence of this great fire, it rotates around it to receive equally in all its parts this preservative virtue. For it would be just as ridiculous to think that this great glowing body turned around some irrelevant point than to imagine that, when we see a roasted skylark, the fireplace must have been rotated around it in order to cook it. Otherwise, if it were the sun's job to carry out this chore, it would seem to follow that medicine needs its patient, that the strong man should bow to the weak man and the great man serve the little man, and that, rather than a ship steering a course around the coasts of a province, the province would need to be moved around the vessel.

"If you find it hard to understand how such a heavy mass can move, then tell me please: are the stars and the heavens that in your view are solid any lighter? Indeed, we are certain that the earth is round, and it is easy for us to conclude from its shape that it moves. But why suppose that the sky is round, since you cannot know this? Yet unless it has this, of all shapes, it certainly cannot move. I have nothing against your eccentrics, your con-centrics or your epicycles,* but when you try to explain them, you fall into confusion – my system does not have this problem. Let us just talk about the natural causes of this movement.

"You are all forced to resort to Intelligences that move and govern your globes. I, however – without disturbing the repose of the Sovereign Being, who has doubtless created nature to be perfect, and whose wisdom has brought it to completeness (so that, having finished it in one way, he did not leave it defective in another), I can find the virtues that make the earth move in the earth itself. So my view is that the sun's rays, together with its influences, strike the earth as they circle round it and make it spin in the same way that we spin a globe by striking it with our hand. The vapours that continually evaporate from the earth on the side where the sun gazes down on it, bounced back by the cold of the middle region, rebound to earth, and, since they have to strike it obliquely, they make it pirouette.

"The explanation of the other two movements is even less complicated: consider, pray..."

At these words, M. de Montmagny interrupted me.

"Please do not bother – I happen to have read a few books by Gassendi on this subject.* Let me tell you what one of our fathers who shared your opinion replied to me one day.

"'Indeed,' he said, 'I can well imagine that the earth turns, not for the reasons put forward by Copernicus, but because the fire of hell, as Holy Scripture teaches us, is enclosed in the centre of the earth, so that the damned trying to flee the heat of the flames climb up against the vault, and thus make the earth turn around, just as a dog makes a wheel turn around when he runs round trapped inside it.'"

We spent some time singing the praises of the good father's zeal, and after pronouncing his panegyric, M. de Montmagny told me that, since Ptolemy's system was so unlikely, he was amazed it was so generally accepted.

"Sir," I replied, "most men judge only by their senses and so yield to the evidence of their eyes. Just as a man whose vessel is sailing along the coast thinks that he is motionless and the shore is moving, men turning with the earth around the sky thought it was the sky itself that was turning around them. Add to that the intolerable pride of human beings, which persuades them that nature has been made for them alone; as if it were likely that the sun, a great body, four hundred and thirty-four times bigger than the earth, had been lit only to ripen our medlars and plumpen our cabbages. As for me, I refuse to go along with the insolence of such brutes, and I believe that the planets are worlds around the sun and that the fixed stars are also suns that have planets around them – worlds that we cannot see from here because they are too small, and their borrowed light cannot reach us.* How can anyone in good faith imagine that such spacious globes are merely great empty fields and that ours, merely because a dozen of us boastful rascals creep around on it, was built to rule over all the rest? What! Just because the sun measures out our days and our years, does that mean that it was made only so that we would not bump our heads against the walls? Not at all: if that visible god sheds light on man, it is by accident, just as the King's torch sheds its light by accident on a housebreaker prowling down the street."*

"But," he replied, "if, as you claim, the fixed stars are all suns, we might conclude that the world is infinite, because it is likely that the peoples on those worlds, turning around a fixed star that you consider to be a sun, are able to see above them even more fixed stars that we cannot see from here: and so on, for ever and ever."

"There is no doubt about it," I replied. "Just as God has made the soul immortal, he has also made the world infinite, if it is true that eternity is nothing other than a boundless length of time and the infinite a limitless extent of space. Furthermore, God himself would be finite if the world were not infinite, since he could not be where there is nothing, and he could not increase the size of the world without adding to his own extent, and starting to be where he had not been before. We can only deduce that, just as we can see Saturn and Jupiter from here, if we were on one or other of those planets, we would be able to view many worlds that are invisible from here and see that the universe is constructed in this way for ever and ever."

"Good Heavens!" he replied. "Whatever you say, I find such an infinity impossible to understand."

"Ah!" I said. "Then tell me – do you understand the nothingness beyond it any better? Not at all. When you think of that nothingness, you can imagine it only to be wind or air, and that is something; but as for the infinite, if you cannot understand it in general, you can at least conceive of it in its parts, since it is not difficult to imagine earth, fire, water, air, stars or the heavens. Now the infinite is nothing other than a boundless interweaving of all those things. If you ask me how these worlds were made, since Holy Scripture speaks of only one world being created by God, my reply is that Scripture speaks of our world merely because it is the only one that God could be bothered to make with his own hands, but all the others that we see or do not see, hanging in the azure of the universe, are nothing other than the foam from suns purging themselves. For how could those great fires subsist if they were not attached to some matter that nourishes them?

"Now just as fire pushes away from itself the ashes choking it, and just as gold in the crucible refines itself by detaching itself from the marcasite that lessens its carat value, and just as we vomit to rid our heart of the indigestible humours that attack it, in just the same way the sun disgorges every day and purges itself of the remains of the matter that nourishes its fire. But when it has completely consumed the matter that sustains it, you can rest assured that it will spread out on every side seeking more fuel, and will batten on all the worlds that it had once made, especially those that happen to be closest; then that great fire, remixing all the bodies, will force them away pell-mell on every side just as before, and having gradually purified itself will start to serve as a sun to those little worlds it engenders by pushing them out of its sphere. It is probably this that led the Pythagoreans to predict the universal conflagration.

"It is not at all ridiculous to imagine this – New France, where we are, provides us with a most convincing example. This vast continent of America is one half of the earth, and yet, in spite of our predecessors who sailed across the ocean a thousand times, it still lay undiscovered; so it was as yet nothing more than a collection of islands, peninsulas and mountains that had arisen on our globe, when the rust from the sun as it cleansed itself was thrust out to a great distance and condensed into relatively heavy balls that were then attracted towards the centre of our world, possibly little by little in tiny particles, but perhaps all at once in one great mass. This is not at all unreasonable: in fact, St Augustine would have applauded it if this country had been discovered during his lifetime; after all, that great personage, whose genius was enlightened by the Holy Spirit, assures us that in his time the earth was as flat as an oven, and swam on the water like one half of a sliced orange. But if I ever have the honour to meet you in France, I will give you my excellent telescope, so that you can observe how certain obscurities that appear as dark patches from here are worlds in the process of construction."

My eyelids were already drooping as I came to the end of my speech, and so M. de Montmagny was obliged to wish me good night. On the next day and the following days we had similar conversations. But since, some time later, the affairs of the province required attention and put a stop to our philosophizing, I returned all the more eagerly to my plan for travelling up to the moon.

As soon as the moon rose, I would go for a walk in the woods, mulling over how to carry out my enterprise successfully. Finally, one day, on Midsummer's Eve, as they were holding council in the fort to decide whether to help the savages of the country against the Iroquois, I went off alone behind our house and up to the summit of a tall hill, and this is what I did there:

With a machine that I had built, imagining it would be able to lift me as high as I wanted, I leapt into the air from the summit of a rock. But since I had miscalculated, I came tumbling back into the valley head over heels. I was badly shaken and went back to my room, but I was not disheartened. I took some ox marrow and rubbed it all over my body, since it was covered with bruises from head to foot, and after fortifying my heart with a bottle of cordial essence, I went back to recover my machine. But it was not there – some soldiers who had been sent into the forest to cut wood to make the scaffolding for the midsummer fire that was to be lit later that evening had chanced to come across it, and had taken it to the fort. They spent some time trying to work out what it could be, and when they had discovered how the mechanism worked, some of them said a number of rockets should be tied round it; these would shoot it up high into the air, and when the mechanism beat its great wings, everyone would take this machine for a fire-dragon.

I spent a long time looking for it and finally found it in the middle of the great square in Quebec just as they were setting fire to it. I was so alarmed at seeing the work of my hands in such great danger that I ran up and seized the arm of the soldier lighting the fuse. I pulled his lit wick away and furiously jumped into my machine to smash the fireworks that had been tied around it, but I was too late, since no sooner had I put both feet into it than I was lifted up into the clouds.

I was filled with the most dreadful horror and panic, but this did not so overwhelm the faculties of my soul as to erase from my memory everything that happened at that moment. So I can tell you that the flame devoured a line of rockets (they had been arranged in sixes, with a fuse running along the edge of every half a dozen), whereupon another tier caught fire and then another, so that the saltpetre as it burst into flames diminished the danger at the same time as it increased it. However, the material was soon all consumed, so that there were no fireworks left, and by the time I was convinced that I would soon be smashing my head on the summit of some mountain, I felt myself (without even moving my body) continuing to rise, and as my machine took leave of me, I saw it fall back to earth.

This amazing turn of events made me swell with such extraordinary joy that, delighted to see myself saved from certain danger, I had the impudence to philosophize about it. So as I looked around, trying to think what could be the cause of this miracle, I saw that my flesh had all puffed up and was still greasy with the marrow that I had smeared over myself to treat the bruises caused by my crash. I realized that, since the moon was on the wane – a phase in which she is accustomed to suck the marrow from animals – she was drinking the marrow I had smeared over myself all the more greedily because her globe was closer to me, and there were no clouds between us to weaken her vigour.

When, according to the calculations I later made, I had travelled much more than three-quarters of the way between earth and moon, I suddenly started falling with my feet uppermost, even though I had not done a somersault. Indeed I would not even have noticed if I had not felt my head charged with the weight of my body. I realized that, in fact, I was not falling back towards our world, for even though I found myself between two moons and was perfectly well aware that I was moving away from the one and approaching the other, I was quite certain that the biggest one was our earth; for, after one or two days' travelling, the distant refractions of the sun had confused the diversity of bodies and climates, and the earth now appeared to me as nothing but a great plate of gold, just like the other body. This led me to imagine that I was descending towards the moon, and I was confirmed in this opinion when I suddenly remembered that I had started to fall only after three-quarters of the distance had been covered.

"This mass weighs less than ours," I thought to myself, "and so the sphere of its activity must also be less extensive. As a result, I felt the force coming from its centre only later."

After falling for a considerable time, as far as I could judge (for the shock of the fall must have prevented me from noticing it), the most I can remember is that I found myself under a tree, all tangled up in three or four quite big branches that had been broken in my fall, and my face spattered with an apple that had squashed against it.

Fortunately, this place was, as you will soon discover, the earthly Paradise, and the tree into which I fell just happened to be the Tree of Life. So, as you can well imagine, without this miraculous turn of events, I would have died a thousand deaths. Since then, I have often reflected on what ordinary people assure us to be true: namely, when you fall from a very high place, you suffocate before reaching the ground, and I have concluded from my adventure that they are quite mistaken – or else that the revitalizing juice of the fruit that had trickled into my mouth had summoned my soul, which was not far away, back into my corpse, still warm and still ready to assume its vital functions.

Indeed, as soon as I had landed, my pain vanished even before it could engrave itself on my memory, and although during my journey I had been greatly vexed by hunger, I now found in its place only a faint remembrance of having ceased to feel hungry.

I picked myself up, and no sooner had I noticed the banks of the widest of the four great rivers that form a lake as they pour out into it than the spirit or invisible soul of the medicinal plants that this country breathes out filled my nostrils with delight. The little pebbles only seemed to be hard and angular: they took care to soften when anyone trod on them.

At first I came across a central crossroads with five avenues radiating off it. It was formed of oak trees that seemed so colossal in height that they held up to the sky a tall parterre of timber. My eyes roamed from their roots to their summits and then back down from their tops to their feet, and I could not decide whether the ground was supporting them or whether they were, rather, carrying the ground suspended from their roots; it seemed as if their superbly lofty brows were being forced to bend under the weight of the celestial globes whose burden they could bear only with a groan. Their arms extended heavenwards and seemed, as they embraced the sky, to be imploring the stars for the pure benevolence of their influence,* drinking it in, before they lost any of their innocence, from the very source of the elements.

Here, on every side, the flowers, which have no gardeners other than nature, breathe out a wild perfume, which stirs and satisfies one's sense of smell; here, the red gleam of a rose on the briar, and the brilliant blue of the violet under the brambles, impel you to judge that they are each more beautiful than the other; here, every season is spring; here, no poisonous plant germinates without its birth displaying its antidote; here, the streams tell the pebbles of their journeys; here, a thousand little winged voices make the forest resound to their songs; and as all these throats together pour out their quivering melodies – they make such general music that every leaf in the wood seems to have taken the tongue and shape of a nightingale. Echo derives so much pleasure from their ditties that, when you hear her repeating their songs, it is as if she wanted to learn them. Next to this wood, two meadows stretch out, whose bright-green grass spreads like an emerald as far as the eye can see. The medley of colours with which spring paints a hundred little flowers mixes and mingles different hues and shades together, and when these flowers toss in the breeze, they seem to be chasing after each other to escape the wind's caress.

This meadow looks like an ocean, but because it is a sea without any shore, my eye, alarmed at having gazed so far without discovering any edge to it, sent my thoughts ranging out across it, and my thoughts, convinced it might be the end of the world, tried to persuade themselves that such a delightful spot had perhaps forced heaven to come down to earth. In the middle of this carpet, so vast and so perfect, there bubbles along the silvery gleam of a rustic fountain whose banks are crowned by a lawn dotted with daisies, buttercups and violets, and those flowers that throng all around seem to be competing as to who will be first to admire her own face in the water. The spring is still in its cradle, having only just been born, and her young polished face is unmarked by a single wrinkle. She twists and turns and retraces her steps countless times, showing that she regrets having to leave her native land; and, as if ashamed of receiving caresses while still with her mother, she repelled with a murmur my playful hand each time it tried to touch her. The animals who came to drink here, more reasonable than those in our world, showed great surprise on seeing that it was broad daylight on the horizon, while they could still see the sun in the Antipodes,* and they barely dared to bend over the bank of the stream for fear of falling into the firmament.

I must confess that, at the sight of so many lovely things, I felt as if I were being tickled by those agreeable pains that they say the embryo feels when its soul is infused into it. My old hair fell out, giving way to new, thicker and looser tresses. I felt my youth reinvigorated, a fresh pink flush in my cheeks, and my natural heat mingling gently with my radical moisture; in fact, I felt a good fourteen years younger.

I had walked for about half a league through a forest of jasmine and myrtle when I saw, lying in the shade, something moving: it was a young adolescent, whose majestic beauty almost impelled me to worship him. He rose to his feet to prevent me.

"It is not to me that you owe your humble devotions, but to God!" he cried.

"You see in me," I replied, "a person bewildered by so many miracles that I do not know which one to admire first. To begin with, coming as I do from a world that you here doubtless consider to be a moon, I thought I had landed in another, which the people in my country also call the moon, and lo and behold, I find myself in paradise, at the feet of a god who refuses to be worshipped, and of a stranger who speaks my language."

"Apart from my being a god," he replied, "what you say is quite true – this earth here is the moon that you can see from your globe, and this place through which you are walking is paradise, but it is the earthly Paradise into which only six people have ever entered: Adam, Eve, Enoch, I (who am the old Elijah), St John the Evangelist and you. You know how the first two were banished from the garden, but you do not know how they reached your world. In fact, once they had both tasted of the forbidden fruit, Adam, fearing that God, angered by his presence, might increase his punishment, considered the moon – your earth – as the sole refuge in which he could take shelter from the pursuit of his Creator.

"Now, in those days, man's imagination was extremely vivid, since it had not yet been corrupted either by debauchery or by the crude nature of his food or by the debilitating effect of illness; so, seized by the violent desire to reach that asylum, and his whole mass having been made lighter by the fire of his enthusiasm, he was raised aloft in the same way that certain philosophers, their imagination sharply focused on one thing, have been lifted into the air, ravished by what you call ecstasy. Eve, rendered weaker and less heated by the infirmity of her sex, would doubtless not have had a vigorous enough imagination to overcome, by the contention of her will, the weight of matter, but since she had only recently been drawn from her husband's body, the sympathy with which her half was still linked to its whole pulled her towards him as he rose, just as amber attracts a straw and just as the magnet turns to the north from which its metal has been taken, and Adam drew up the work of his rib, just as the sea draws the rivers that have emerged from it. Once they had reached your earth, they settled between Mesopotamia and Arabia; the Hebrews knew the man by the name of Adam, and the idolaters called him Prometheus, whom their poets feigned had stolen the fire of heaven, because the descendants he engendered were endowed with a soul as perfect as the one with which God had filled him.

"So the first man, going off to dwell in your world, left this one empty, but the All-Wise did not wish such a happy seat to remain uninhabited: a few centuries later he permitted Enoch, tired of the company of men whose innocence was growing corrupt, to feel a wish to leave their company. But this holy man judged that there was no retreat safe enough from the ambition of his forebears who were already slaughtering one another as they divided up your world between them – no world apart from the blessed land of which Adam, his ancestor, long ago had told him so much. But how could he reach it? Jacob's ladder had not yet been invented! The grace of the Highest provided the solution: it led Enoch to realize that the fire of heaven came down onto the holocausts of the just and of those who were agreeable in the sight of the Lord, in accordance with the words of his mouth: 'The odour of the sacrifices of the just has risen up to me.'*

"One day, as this divine flame was busily consuming a victim that Enoch was offering to the Eternal, he filled two great vessels with the vapour coming off it and sealed them hermetically with luting, then he tied them under his armpits. Immediately the smoke, which naturally rose straight up to God, and could only by miracle penetrate metal, pushed the vessels aloft, and carried that holy man with them. When he had risen up to the moon and cast his eyes on this lovely garden, he felt faint with an almost supernatural feeling of joy, and thereby realized that this was the earthly Paradise where his forefather had once lived. He quickly untied the vessels that he had fixed like wings to his shoulders, and did so with such skill that he was hardly four fathoms in the air above the moon when he bade farewell to his floats. He was still high enough up, however, to have been severely wounded had he not been wearing a great robe that ballooned out in the wind, and had it not been for the ardour of the fire of charity that supported him as well. As for the vessels, they continued to rise until God set them in the sky, and they are what you today call the Balances, or Libra, which show us every day that they are still filled with the odours from the sacrifice of a just man, by the favourable influences that they inspire on the horoscope of Louis the Just,* who had Libra in the ascendant.

"But he had not yet reached this garden – he arrived here only some time later. It was when the Flood overflowed, for the waters under which your world was submerged rose to such a prodigious height that the ark sailed through the sky right next to the moon. Humans could see this globe through the window, but the reflection of this great opaque body grew weaker as, being so close, they shared its light, and each of them thought that it was a part of the earth that had not been flooded. There was only one daughter of Noah, Achab* by name, who – perhaps

17

because she had realized that, as their ship rose, they were getting closer to this heavenly body – maintained with all her might that it was definitely the moon. However much they protested that when they took soundings they measured only fifteen cubits of water, she replied that the sounding lead must have bumped into the back of a whale that they had mistaken for land; for her part, she was quite convinced that it was the moon in person on which they were about to land. Finally, since everyone shares the ideas of people who are similar to themselves, all the other women chimed in with her view. So, despite being forbidden by the men, they started to put a little skiff out to sea. Achab was the most daring, so she wanted to be the first to risk the danger. She gaily leapt aboard, and all those of her sex were about to join her, until a wave separated the little boat from the ship. They shouted after her for all they were worth, they repeatedly called her a lunatic, protesting that she would be the reason why one day all women would be reproached for having a quarter of the moon in their heads: she simply laughed at them.

"And so she floated out of the world. The animals followed her example, since most of the birds who felt their wings strong enough to risk the voyage, having been so trammelled by the first prison in which their freedom had ever been pent up, took flight too. Even some of the braver quadrupeds started swimming. Nearly a thousand of them had left before the sons of Noah were able to close the stable doors that the throng of escaping animals had pushed open. Most of them reached this new world. As for the skiff, it came aground on a very pleasant hilltop where the noble Achab climbed out and, highly delighted to have discovered that this land was indeed the moon, refused to re-embark and join her brothers.

"She settled down for a while in a grotto, and one day, as she was out walking and trying to decide whether she was sad or, in fact, perfectly happy to have lost the company of her family, she noticed a man knocking down acorns. She was so overjoyed to meet him that she ran over to embrace him; her embraces were reciprocated, since it had been even longer since the old man had seen a human face. It was Enoch the Just. They lived together, and if it had not been for the impiety of his children and the pride of his wife, which forced him to retire into the woods, they would have managed to live out their days together with all the sweetness that God showers on the marriage of the just.

"Here, every day, in the wildest retreats of those savage and awesome solitudes, that good old man, with a purified spirit, gave his heart as a burnt offering to God. Then, one day, an apple from the Tree of Knowledge that – as you know – is found in this garden, dropped into the river by the side of which the tree was planted. The apple was borne at the mercy of the waves outside Paradise to a place where poor Enoch, to sustain his life, used to catch fish. This fine fruit was caught in his net, and he ate it. Immediately he knew where the earthly Paradise was, and, thanks to secrets that you cannot conceive if you have not eaten of the apple of knowledge, as he had, he came to live here.

"Now I must tell you how I came here. I am sure you have not forgotten that my name is Elijah, as I told you just now. Anyway, I was in your world, living with Elisha, a Hebrew like myself, on the banks of the Jordan. I passed my days in the midst of books, leading a life that was so sweet that I did not even regret the way the days flowed by. However, the more my spirit was illumined by knowledge, the more it also realized how much knowledge it lacked. Whenever our priests reminded me of Adam, the memory of the perfect philosophy that he had possessed made me yearn to possess it in turn. I despaired of ever being able to acquire it; then, one day, after sacrificing to expiate the sins of my mortal being, I went to sleep, and the Angel of the Lord appeared to me in a dream. As soon as I was awake, I immediately started to carry out the activities he had prescribed for me – I took a magnet about two feet square and placed it in the furnace, then, when it was completely purged, precipitated and dissolved, I drew out the attractive part, calcined the whole elixir and reduced it to a piece about as thick as a medium-sized ball.

"After these preparations, I constructed a chariot of very light iron and when, a few months later, all the parts of the contrivance were ready, I climbed aboard my industrious cart. You may well ask me what all this machinery was for – know then that the angel had told me in a dream that if I wanted to acquire a perfect science as I desired, I should rise to the world of the moon, where I would find the Paradise of Adam and the Tree of Knowledge, and as soon as I had tasted of its fruit, my soul would be illumined with all the truths of which a creature is capable. This, then, was the journey for which I built my chariot. Finally I climbed aboard, and when I was sitting firmly and comfortably on the seat, I flung my magnetic ball high into the air. Now the iron machine, which I had forged so as to be more massive in the middle than at the extremities, was immediately raised aloft and in perfect balance, since it always rose more quickly by its middle. So I could arrive where the magnet attracted me, and as soon as I had risen high enough to catch up with it, my hand would fling it even higher."

"But," I interrupted, "how did you throw your ball so directly above your chariot that it never fell to the side?"

"There is nothing particularly wonderful about that," he said, "since the magnet, being flung into the air, attracted the iron straight to itself, and so it was impossible for me ever to rise to one side or other of it. True, even when I was holding my ball, I never stopped rising, as the chariot continued to chase after the magnet as I held it above it; but the iron machine rose so swiftly and vigorously to catch up with my ball that it made my body concertina together – so this was an experiment I tried only once. In fact, it was an amazing sight to see, for I had polished the steel of this flying house so carefully that it reflected the sun's light on every side, so brightly and dazzlingly that I thought I was being swept aloft in a chariot of fire.* Finally, after throwing it up and flying after it many times over, I eventually reached, like you, the point at which I started to fall towards this world, and because at this moment I was holding my ball tightly in my hands, my chariot, the seat of which pressed into me in its attempt to catch up with the attractive metal, did not let me go; my only fear was that I would break my neck, but to protect myself, I threw my ball back from time to time, so that my machine felt itself naturally re-attracted, rested for a while and thereby broke the force of my fall. Finally, when I saw that I was just two or three hundred fathoms away from the ground, I threw my ball on every side level with the chariot, sometimes this way, sometimes that, until my eyes could see the garden clearly. I immediately threw the ball down towards it, and, as my machine followed it, I allowed myself to fall until I could see that I would land on sand, and then I threw it just one foot above my head, and that little throw immediately cushioned the impact that the fall had given it, so that I landed no more violently than if I had simply fallen from my own height.

"I will not attempt to depict the amazement with which I was filled by my encounter with the marvels of this place, because it was quite similar to the amazement which I have just seen overcome you. I will simply say that, the very next day, I came across the Tree of Life, by means of which I stop myself getting old. It soon consumed the serpent and breathed it out in clouds of smoke."

At these words I said to him:

"Venerable and holy patriarch, I would be most happy to know what you mean by that serpent who was consumed."

He smiled and replied to me in these terms:

"I was forgetting, my son, that I should reveal to you a secret that you cannot be expected to know. Well, after Eve and her husband had eaten of the forbidden apple, God, to punish the serpent who had tempted them with it, banished him into the body of the man. Ever since then, there has been no human creature who, as a punishment for the crime of his first father, does not nurse a serpent in his body that is descended from that first one. You call this serpent the bowels, and you think the bowels are necessary for the functions of life, but I must tell you that they are nothing else than serpents coiled and twisted over and against themselves. When you hear your entrails crying, it is the serpent hissing, and, following the gluttonous nature with which it once incited the first man to eat too much, it demands to eat as well, for God, wishing to chastise you, wanted to make you mortal like the other animals, and therefore made you obsessed by this insatiable creature, so that if you gave it too much to eat, you would choke. And if, when the famished creature gnaws your stomach with its invisible teeth, you refuse to give it its pittance, it cries out, it rages, it disgorges the poison that your doctors call bile, and inflames you so much, by the venom with which it floods your arteries, that you are soon consumed by it. Finally, to demonstrate to you that your bowels are serpents in your body, remember that, in the tombs of Aesculapius, Scipio, Alexander, Charles Martel and Edward of England, serpents were found still feeding on the corpses of their hosts."*

"Indeed," I said interrupting him, "I noticed how that serpent is always trying to escape from men's bodies: you can see its head and neck emerging from under our bellies. But also, God did not permit man alone to be tormented by it; he decided that the serpent would rise erect against a woman to spit its poison into her and that she would swell up for nine months after it had pricked her. And to show you that I am speaking in accordance with the word of the Lord, he told the serpent when he cursed it that, however much it made the woman stumble when it rose against her, she would eventually make it bow its head."*

I was about to continue spouting these facetious tales, but Elijah stopped me.

"Remember," he said, "that this place is holy."

He fell silent for a while, as if bringing back to remembrance the place where he had lived, and then he resumed as follows:

"I taste of the fruit of life only once every hundred years; its juice has a taste rather like that of spirit of wine; it was, I believe, the apple that Adam had eaten that led to our first fathers living for so long, since into their seed had flowed something of its energy, until this energy was finally extinguished in the waters of the Flood. The Tree of Knowledge is planted opposite. Its fruit is covered by a rind that produces ignorance in anyone who tastes of it, and under the thick peel it preserves the spiritual virtues of this learned food. In bygone days, God, after exiling Adam from this blessed land, rubbed his gums with its rind in case he managed to find his way back. Thereafter he spent over fifteen years talking nonsense, and forgot everything so completely that neither he nor his descendants, down to the time of Moses, even remembered the Creation. But the remaining strength of the thick and heavy rind was finally dissipated by the fire and clarity of that great prophet's genius. Fortunately, I addressed myself to one of those apples that was ripe enough for its skin to have fallen off, and hardly had my saliva moistened it than universal philosophy absorbed me. It was as if an infinite number of little eyes had plunged into my head, and I was able to speak with the Lord. When I later reflected on this miraculous ravishment, I really thought that I could not have vanquished, by the occult virtues of a mere natural body, the vigilance of the Seraph that God had set to guard this Paradise. But since it pleases him to use secondary causes, I thought he had inspired me with the idea of this means of entry, just as he wanted to use Adam's ribs to make a wife for him, even though he could have formed her from earth as he had formed Adam.

"I stayed in this garden for a long while, wandering around companionless. But finally, since the Angel who was the door-keeper of the place was my principal host, I felt a desire to greet him. My journey was done in an hour's walk, since at the end of this time I reached a part of the country where a thousand flashes of lightning fused together into one, forming a blinding dazzle that served only to make the darkness visible.

"I had still not recovered from this surprise when I saw before me a handsome adolescent.

"'I am,' he said, 'the archangel you seek; I have just read in God that he has suggested the means for you to come here and that he desired you to await his wishes.'

"He talked to me of several things, including the following: the light by which I appeared to have been so alarmed was not all that terrible; it was lit up almost every evening, when he was doing his rounds, because – so as to avoid being taken by surprise by the wizards who enter everywhere without being seen – he was obliged to brandish his fiery two-handed sword all around the earthly Paradise, and that light was produced by the flashes of his steel blade.

"'The flashes of lightning that you can see from your world,' he added, 'are produced by me. If you sometimes see them from far away, this is because the clouds of a distant climate, being disposed to receive this impression, transmit these flickering images of fire to you, just as a vapour in another position will sometimes form a rainbow. I will not tell you any more, and in any case, the apple of knowledge is not far from here; as soon as you have eaten of it, you will be as learned as I am. But above all, guard yourself against error – most of the fruits hanging from this vegetable are surrounded by a rind, and if you taste that rind, you will descend to a level lower than man, while the inside will make you rise as high as an angel.'"

This is the point Elijah had reached in describing the instructions the seraph had given him when a little man came up to join us.

"This is the same Enoch I told you about," my guide whispered to me.

As he was speaking, Enoch presented us with a basket full of certain fruits similar to pomegranates that he had just discovered that very same day in a distant grove. On Elijah's command, I stuffed some of them into my pockets, and then Enoch asked Elijah who I was.

"That is an adventure that deserves to be narrated at greater length," replied my guide. "When we have retired for the evening, he himself will relate to us the miraculous details of his journey."

* * *

After these words, we arrived at a kind of hermitage made of palm branches ingeniously woven together with myrtles and orange branches. Here, in a little nook, I spotted piles of a floss silk so white and airy that it could have passed for the soul of snow. I also saw spindles scattered around here and there. I asked my guide what they were used for.

"To spin with," he told me. "When our friend Enoch wishes to relax from his meditation, sometimes he dresses this rough material, sometimes he spins thread from it, and sometimes he weaves cloth, which is then used to run up shirts for the eleven thousand virgins.* In your world, you must occasionally have come across a certain white stuff that floats around in autumn, at harvest time – the peasants call it 'Our Lady's cotton'* – it is actually the flock that Enoch combs out of his flax as he cards it."

We did not stay long before taking our leave of Enoch, who lived in this hut as in his cell: what obliged us to leave so soon was the fact that, every six hours, he says his prayers, and this period of time had now elapsed since his last orisons.

As we went along, I begged Elijah to finish the story of the assumptions that he had already started, and told him that, if memory served me aright, he had got as far as the assumption of Saint John the Evangelist.*

"Well," he replied, "if you do not have enough patience to wait for the apple of knowledge to teach you all these things better than I can, I will do so myself. Know then that God…"

At this word, the Devil must have interfered somehow or other, as I could not hold back a mocking remark.

"I remember," I interrupted him, "one day, God noticed that the soul of this Evangelist was starting to become so detached from his body that he could only keep it in by clenching his teeth, and yet the hour at which he was due to be swept up here had almost arrived. So, as God had not had time to prepare a machine for him, he had no choice but to make him suddenly arrive here at his journey's end without actually having to make the journey."

If looks could kill, Elijah would have slain me with his stare
– if I had been in a state to die of anything but hunger.

"That is a foul thing to say!" he replied, recoiling from me.
"You have the impudence to make mockery of holy things! Do
not think you would get away with it, if the Almighty did not
wish to leave to the nations of the earth a memorable example of his mercy. Go, impious man! Away from here! Go and
publish abroad, both in this world and the other – for you are
predestined to return there – the irreconcilable hatred that God
bears towards atheists."

Hardly had he uttered this imprecation than he seized hold
of me and pushed me towards the gate. When we came to a
tall tree whose fruit-laden branches were bent almost to the
ground, he told me:

"Here is the Tree of Knowledge, from which you would have
derived unimaginable enlightenment if you had not been so
impious."

No sooner had he spoken than, pretending that I was feeling
faint and weak, I allowed myself to fall against a branch from
which I adroitly stole an apple. I still needed to take just a few
strides before I could set foot outside this delightful park, but
I was so overcome by the pangs of hunger that I quite forgot
I was in the hands of a wrathful prophet. As a result, I pulled
out one of those apples that I had stuffed into my pocket, and
sank my teeth into it, but instead of taking one of the apples
that Enoch had given me, my hand fell on the apple that I had
picked from the Tree of Knowledge: unfortunately, I had not
peeled it yet.

No sooner had I tasted it than a dense cloud fell over my soul:
I could no longer see my apple, nor Elijah at my side, and in the
whole hemisphere my eyes could not recognize a single trace
of the earthly Paradise. And yet in spite of all this, I could still
remember everything that had happened to me. Whenever I
have since reflected on this miracle, I have decided that the peel
of this apple had not entirely stupefied me, since my teeth had

bitten right through it and tasted a little of the juice inside it: the energy of this juice had dissipated the bad effects of the peel.

I was quite surprised to find myself alone in the middle of a country that I did not know at all. However much I gazed round at the countryside on all sides, no creature offered itself to console my gaze. Finally I decided to start walking until Fortune led me into the company of some beast, or else of Death.

Fortune heard my prayer, for after an eighth of a league I encountered two very large animals, one of which halted in front of me, while the other bounded back to its lair (at least, this is what I deduced when, some time later, I saw it returning accompanied by over seven or eight hundred creatures of the same species that thronged around me). When I saw them from closer up, I realized that they had the same shape, size and face as we do. This adventure reminded me of the fairy tales my nurse had once told me about sirens, fauns and satyrs. From time to time they emitted such furious howls – doubtless caused by their immense surprise on seeing me – that I thought I too must have turned into some kind of monster.

One of those man-beasts seized me by the scruff of my neck, like a wolf seizing hold of a sheep, tossed me onto its back, and carried me off to their city. I was quite amazed, when I realized that they were men, to see that every one of them walked on all fours.

When the people saw me pass by, and observed that I was so small (for most of them are twelve cubits long), and my body was supported by just two legs, they refused to believe that I was a man, since it was their belief, among other things, that as nature had given both men and beasts two arms and two legs, men ought to use these limbs the same way that they did. And indeed, mulling over this subject since then, I have often reflected that this bodily posture was not at all eccentric, bearing in mind that our children, when their only teacher is still nature, walk on all fours, and raise themselves onto two legs only thanks to their nurses, who train them in little chariots, and attach leashes to them to prevent them falling on all fours, a position in which our bodily mass tends to repose.

And so they commented (as I later found out from an interpreter) that I must indubitably be the female of the Queen's pet animal. As such (or for some other reason) I was taken straight to the town hall, where I realized from the buzz of voices and the gestures made by the people and the magistrates that they were debating together what I might be. When they had conferred for a long time, a certain citizen who looked after rare animals requested the aldermen to hand me over to him until the Queen sent for me to go and live with my male.

Nobody raised any difficulties, and this mountebank took me to his home, where he taught me to play the fool, to turn somersaults and pull faces, and in the afternoons he stood at the door taking money from people who wished to see me perform. Finally Heaven, moved by my plight and angered by the sight of its master's temple being profaned, decreed that, one day when I was tied to the end of a rope with which the charlatan made me jump to amuse the inquisitive throng, one of those watching stared at me attentively for a while and then asked me, in Greek, who I was. I was amazed to hear someone talking one of the languages of our world. He questioned me for a while; I answered him, and went on to give him a general account of the whole enterprise and outcome of my journey. He consoled me, and I remember him saying:

"Well, my son, you are finally paying the penalty for the failings of your world. There is a vulgar mob here, just as there, which cannot stand the thought of things to which it is not accustomed. But bear in mind that you are simply being treated fairly, for if anyone from this land were to rise up to yours and make so bold as to call himself a man, your doctors would have him strangled as a monster or as a monkey possessed by the Devil."

He went on to promise me that he would alert the Court to the disaster that had befallen me; he added that the minute he had set eyes on me, his heart had told him that I was a man, since he had once travelled to the world from which I came; my country was the moon, I was a Gaul and he had long ago lived in Greece; he was called "Socrates' demon",* and since the death of that philosopher he had been the governor and tutor of Epaminondas in Thebes. Then, having settled among the Romans, justice had led him to join the party of Cato the Younger, after whose death he had sided with Brutus.* All those great personages, he continued, had left nothing behind them in the world but the image of their virtues, and so he had withdrawn with his companions, sometimes into the temples, sometimes into isolated spots.

"Finally," he added, "the people in your world became so stupid and coarse that my companions and I lost any pleasure we had once had in educating them. You must have heard of us – we were called oracles, nymphs, genies, fairies, gods of the hearth, lemurs, larvae, lamiae, hobgoblins, naiads, incubi, shades, manes, spectres and phantoms, and we abandoned your world in the reign of Augustus, shortly after I had appeared to Drusus, son of Livia, who was waging war in Germany, forbidding him to go any further.* I returned from there only recently, for the second time. A hundred years ago, I was commissioned to travel there, and I wandered all around Europe and conversed with various people whom you may possibly know. One day, I appeared to Cardano as he was studying; I informed him of a great many things, and in recompense he promised me that he would bear witness to posterity of who it was that had inspired him with the marvellous things he was going to write. I there saw Agrippa, the Abbé Tritème, Doctor Faust, La Brosse and César, as well as a certain cabal of young men known to ordinary folk by the name of "Knights of the Rosy Cross", to whom I taught several tricks and natural secrets, which will no doubt have enabled them to pass among the people for great magicians.* I also knew Campanella;* I was the one who, during his detention by the Inquisition in Rome, taught him to copy, in face and body, the usual grimaces and postures of those whose inner thoughts

he needed to know, so that, by adopting the same pose, he would
arouse in himself the thoughts that this pose had summoned
up in the minds of his adversaries. In this way, knowing their
innermost thoughts, he would be able to deal with them better.
At my request, he started to write a book that we entitled *De
sensu rerum*.* I also frequented, in France, La Mothe Le Vayer
and Gassendi.* The latter of these is a man who writes as a
philosopher, just as the former is a man who lives that role. I
also made the acquaintance of several other men whom your
age hails as "divine", but I found nothing in them but a great
deal of empty chatter and considerable pride.

"Finally, as I was crossing over from your country into England
to study the manners and customs of its inhabitants, I met a man
who is the shame of his native land – for it must be a source of
shame to the great men of your State, who recognize the virtue
of which he is the throne, and yet do not revere it. I will cut short
my encomium of his qualities and merely say that he is full of
spirit and passion, and if ascribing both these qualities (one of
which would have sufficed to distinguish a hero in bygone days)
to a single person were not enough to tell you his name – Tristan
l'Hermite* – I would have refrained from naming him, since I
am sure he will not forgive such an indiscretion. But since I do
not expect ever to return to your world, I can bear witness to the
truth for my conscience's sake. Truly, I have to say that when I
saw such lofty virtue, I was afraid it would not be recognized;
that is why I tried to persuade him to accept three vials. The first
was full of talcum oil, the second contained powder of projec-
tion, and the third potable gold – that vegetable salt from which
your philosophers promise eternity.* But he refused them with
a more noble disdain than Diogenes refusing the compliments
of Alexander when he came to visit him in his barrel.* Anyway,
I can add nothing to the praise of this great man other than
this: he is the only poet, the only philosopher and the only free
man that you have among you. Those then are the important
personages with whom I conversed; all the others, at least those

I knew, fall so far below the human level that I have seen beasts of somewhat more distinction.

"In any case, I am not a native of your earth, nor of this one; I was born on the sun. But since it occasionally happens that our world becomes overpopulated, because of the long lifespan of its inhabitants, and because it is practically free of wars and illnesses, from time to time our magistrates send out colonies into the worlds around us. As for myself, I was ordered to go to earth, where I was declared head of the tribe that was sent along with me. I later moved to this world, for the reasons I have given you, and if I am still here and have not left, it is because here the men are lovers of truth. There are no pedants; philosophers are persuaded by reason alone; and the authority of a scholar, or of the greatest number, is of no greater weight than that of a corn-thresher, if the latter's powers of reasoning are as good. In short, in this country, the only people who are deemed to be out of their minds are the sophists and the orators."

I asked him how long they lived for on the sun. He told me: "Three or four thousand years."

And he continued:

"To make myself visible as I am at present, when I sense that the corpse in which I dwell is almost worn out, or when the organs can no longer perform their functions so perfectly, I breathe my way into the young body of someone recently dead.

"Even though the inhabitants of the sun are not as numerous as those of this world, the sun nonetheless is often overcrowded, because the people there, being of a very hot temperament, are restless, ambitious and always hungry for more.

"This should not come as much of a surprise to you: after all, although our globe is very huge and yours is small, and although we die only after four thousand years, and you after half a century, all the same I can tell you that, just as there are not so many pebbles as there is earth, not so many insects as there are plants, not so many animals as there are insects, nor so many men as there are animals, in the same way, there cannot be so many demons as there are men, because of the difficulties encountered in reproducing such a perfect composition."

I asked him whether they were of bodily form like us; yes, he replied, they were of bodily form – though not like us, nor like anything that we consider such, because we commonly call "body" only that which can be touched; furthermore there was nothing in nature that was not material, and, although they themselves were material, they were constrained, when they wanted to appear to us, to assume bodies in proportion with what our senses are capable of experiencing. I assured him that what had convinced many people that the stories told about them were merely an effect of the dreams of the simple-minded was the way they appeared only at night. He replied that, since they were obliged to construct for themselves the bodies that they needed rather hastily, they often only had time to make these bodies capable of appearing to one sense alone: sometimes hearing, as in the voices of oracles; sometimes sight, as in will-o'-the-wisps and spectres; and sometimes touch, as with incubi and nightmares. Since this mass was merely air, thickened in one way or another, light destroyed these bodies through its heat, just as we see light dissipating fog by dilating it.

All these fascinating things he explained to me made me curious to question him about his birth and his death: whether in the land of the sun the individual came into being through the processes of generation, and whether he died through the disorder of his temperament or the breakdown of his organs.

"There is too little relation," he said, "between your senses and the explanation of these mysteries. You people imagine that what you cannot understand is either spiritual or nonexistent – this reasoning is quite false, but it is evidence of the fact that in the universe there are perhaps a million things that, in order to be known, would require in us a million organs, all completely different. Take me, for example: through my senses I can conceive the cause of the sympathy that the magnet has with the pole, the ebbing of the sea and what happens to an animal after death; your minds do not stretch so far because your ideas are disproportionate with these miracles, just as someone blind from birth cannot imagine the beauty of the landscape, the colours of a painting or the tints of the rainbow. Or else he will imagine them sometimes as something palpable, sometimes as something edible, sometimes as a sound, sometimes as an odour. Likewise, if I tried to explain to you what I perceive through the senses that you lack, you would imagine them as something which can be heard, seen, touched, smelt or tasted – and yet it is nothing of the kind."

This is the point he had reached when my mountebank realized that the audience was starting to get bored, since they could not understand the language we were speaking, which they took to be mere inarticulate grunting; he started to tug at my rope even harder so as to make me jump, and all the spectators had their fill of laughter, proclaiming that I had almost as much of a mind as the beasts of their country; whereupon they made their way home.

In this way the harshness of the mistreatment meted out to me by my master was softened by the visits of that obliging demon. As for conversing with other people, apart from the fact that they took me for an animal firmly fixed in the category of brute beasts, I did not know their language, and they did not understand mine, so you can guess how well suited we were. In fact, there are two types of language used in that country: one serves the nobles, while the other is peculiar to the people.

That of the nobles is nothing but a melody of inarticulate tones somewhat similar to our music when words have not been added. And to be sure, it is an invention that is both very useful and very agreeable, for when they are tired of speaking, or when they disdain to prostitute their throats to that usage, they sometimes take up a lute, and sometimes another instrument, which they use as well as they use their voices to communicate their thoughts; as a result there will sometimes be fifteen or twenty people gathered together debating some vexatious point of theology or the difficult points of a trial, all in the form of the most harmonious concert with which the ear can be tickled.

The second language, the one used by the people, is expressed by a quivering of the limbs – but not perhaps the way you might imagine, for certain parts of the body signify a whole speech. For example, moving a finger, a hand, an ear, a lip, an arm or a cheek, each by itself constitutes a prayer or a whole sentence with all its clauses. Other movements serve merely to designate words: a furrow on the brow, for instance, various ripples of the muscles, a bending back of the hands, a stamping of the feet, a twisting of the arms; as a result, while they are speaking, given their habit of walking about entirely naked, their limbs, accustomed to gesticulating their ideas, move about so violently that it does not seem to be a man speaking, but a body shaking.

Almost every day the demon paid me a visit, and his marvellous conversation enabled me to endure the violence of my captivity without tedium. Finally, one day, I saw a strange man coming into my lodgings. He licked me for some considerable time, then gently picked me up in his jaws under my armpit and, with one of his paws supporting me so that I would not be hurt, threw me across his back, and I found myself sitting so comfortably and so much at my ease that, despite my mortification at finding myself treated like a beast, I had no desire to escape – and in any case, those men who walk on all fours go much more swiftly than we do, since even the heaviest of them can catch a running stag.

I was, however, extremely despondent at not having any news of my courteous demon, and on the evening of the first day's journey, once I had arrived at a lodging, I walked up and down in the inn yard waiting for the meal to be ready, when along came my carrier. He was very young and rather handsome; he came up, laughed in my face and threw his two front feet round my neck. I stared at him for a while, and then he said to me, in French:

"What's this? Don't you recognize your old friend?"

I will leave you to imagine the feelings that then overwhelmed me. To be sure, my surprise was so great that I started to think the whole globe of the moon – everything that had happened to me there, and everything that I saw – was the result of some magic spell. But that man-beast who had served as my mount continued to talk to me.

"You had promised me that you would never forget the favours I did you."

I vigorously protested that I had never seen him.

Finally he said to me:

"I am the demon of Socrates who kept you company during the time you were in prison. I left yesterday as I promised you, to go and alert the King to your mishap, and I travelled three hundred leagues in eighteen hours, arriving here at midday to wait for you, but..."

"But," I interrupted him, "how can that be possible, seeing that yesterday you were extremely long while today you are very short; yesterday you had a weak and broken voice while today your voice is clear and strong; and yesterday you were a grey-haired old man, while today you are still young? Good Heavens! In my country we travel from birth to death – can it be that the animals in this country go from death to birth, and that you grow younger as you grow older?"

"As soon as I spoke of you to the Prince," he said to me, "no sooner had I received the order to bring you than I felt the body in which I was dwelling so weary and exhausted that all its organs refused to perform their functions. I asked which way it was to the hospital, and made my way there. As soon as I entered the first room, I found a young man who had just breathed his last. I approached the body, and, pretending I had seen it moving slightly, I protested to all those present that he was not dead, that his illness was not even dangerous – and adroitly, without being noticed, I breathed my way into his body. My old corpse immediately fell to the ground; meanwhile, I arose in the shape of this young man; everyone cried, 'It's a miracle!' and, without staying to argue, I swiftly went off to find your mountebank, where I picked you up."

He would have told me more if people had not come to fetch us for dinner; my guide led me into a magnificently furnished room, but I did not see any food prepared. Such a dismaying absence of meat, when I was dying of starvation, obliged me to ask him where the table was laid. But I did not hear what he replied, for three or four young boys, the host's children, immediately came up to me and with great politeness stripped me down to my underwear. This unusual ritual so amazed me that I did not even dare to ask the reason from my handsome attendants, and, I do not know how, when my guide asked me what I would like for starters, I just managed to utter these two words: "some soup". Immediately I smelt the fragrance of the most succulent broth that ever assailed the nose of Dives. I tried to rise from my seat and follow my nose to the source of this delightful vapour, but my carrier stopped me, saying:

"Where do you think you're off to? We'll be going out for a walk a little later, but now it's time to eat, so finish your soup and then the next course will arrive."

"And where the devil is this soup?" I angrily retorted. "Have you bet someone that you will be able to spend the whole day pulling my leg?"

"I thought," he replied, "that in the city we have just come from, you would have seen your master, or someone else, taking his meals – that's why I hadn't mentioned the way we eat in this country. So, since you still haven't realized, you need to know that here we live only on vapour. The art of cookery consists in gathering the exhalations that rise from meat into large, specially moulded vessels; several different sorts of these vapours are gathered to suit different tastes, depending on the appetites of the dinner guests, and the vessel containing this odour is uncorked; then another is opened, and then another, and so on, until the company has eaten its fill. Unless you have already lived in this way, you will never be able to believe that one's nose, even without teeth or throat, can perform the office of a man's mouth to feed him – but I will now demonstrate as much to you."

No sooner had he finished speaking than I smelt so many delicious and nourishing vapours wafting successively into the room that in less than a half-quarter of an hour I felt completely full. We rose from table and he said:

"This is not something that ought to cause you a great deal of wonder, since you cannot have lived for so long without observing that in your world the kitchen cooks and pastry cooks, although they eat less than persons of other professions, are still much fatter than they are. Where do their plump bellies come from if not from the vapour rising from the meat with which they are always surrounded, seeping into their bodies and nourishing them? So it is that the people in this world enjoy a much more consistent and vigorous good health, because their food barely creates any excrement, which is the cause of almost every illness. You might have been surprised to find yourself being undressed before the meal, since this custom is never employed in your country, but it is the way we do things here, and ensures that the animal is more permeable to the vapour."

"Sir," I replied, "there is a great deal of plausibility in what you say, and I myself have just experienced some of its effects, but I must confess that, being unable to de-brutalize myself so quickly, I would be really happy to sink my teeth into something nice and solid."

He promised he would find something – but it would only be for the next day because, he said, eating so soon after a meal might give me a touch of indigestion. We continued to converse for a while, then went up to our room to get ready for bed.

At the top of the stairs a man presented himself to us, and, after scrutinizing us for some time, he took me into a small room whose floor was covered with orange flowers to a depth of three feet, while he led my demon into another filled with carnations and jasmines. When he saw how amazed I seemed to be at this magnificence, he told me that this was the type of bed used here. Finally we each lay down in our respective little chambers, and as soon as I had stretched out on my flowers, I saw by the light of some thirty or so big glow-worms contained in a jar (for they use no candles) the same three or four young boys who had undressed me at dinner. One of them started to tickle my feet, and one my thighs, and one my hips, and another my arms – all of them so charmingly and delicately that in less than a moment I felt myself drowsing off to sleep.

The following day I saw my demon entering with the sunlight.

"I've kept my word," he told me. "You'll have a more substantial breakfast than your dinner yesterday."

At these words I got up and he led me by the hand to a place behind the garden where one of the host's children was waiting for us, holding a weapon that looked rather like one of our rifles. He asked my guide if I would like a dozen larks, since baboons (and he thought I was one such) fed on that meat. Hardly had I replied "yes" than the hunter fired a shot into the air, and twenty or thirty larks fell to our feet ready cooked. "Imagine that!" I thought to myself. "We have a proverb in our world about a country where larks fall to the ground ready roasted! Somebody must have gone there from here to tell us."

"Just eat," my demon told me. "They have invented a way of mixing the ingredients needed to season the game together with the gunpowder, which kills, plucks and roasts it."

I picked up some of the larks and, taking his word for it, tucked in: and indeed, I have never tasted anything so delicious in all my life.

After this breakfast we got ready to leave, and, making a thousand grimaces of the kind they use when they want to show affection, the host was given a paper by my demon. I asked him if he were settling the bill. "No," he replied: he owed our host nothing – these were some lines of poetry.

"Poetry?" I exclaimed. "So tavern-keepers are connoisseurs of poetry, are they?"

"It is the currency of this country," he told me, "and the expenses we incurred here amounted to a sixain,* which I have just given him. I was not afraid of being short of money – even if we were to fill our faces here for a whole week, we would not spend so much as a sonnet, and I have four of those with me, together with two epigrams, two odes and an eclogue."

"Aha!" I thought to myself. "That's exactly the same currency that Sorel makes Hortensius use in *Francion* – I remember it clearly.* He obviously stole the idea from here – but who the devil can he have learnt it from? It must have been his mother: I've heard she was a lunatic."

I then asked my demon if these poems continued to be valid currency as often as they were copied out. "No," he replied, and continued:

"When an author has composed a piece of poetry, he takes it to the Royal Mint, where the appointed poets of the kingdom hold their sessions. There the official versifiers assay the pieces, and, if they are judged to be of good alloy, they are valued not according to their weight but according to their wit, and in this way, when someone dies of hunger, it means that he is a blockhead: men of wit can always eat their fill."

I was filled with rapture and admiration at the judicious policy of this country and he continued:

"There are other people who run their inns quite differently. When you're about to leave, they ask you for a note of hand to be paid in the next world, equivalent to the costs, and once you have given it to them, they write down, in a great register that they call God's Account Book, an entry of this kind: 'Item, the value of so many verses delivered on such a day to such a person: God must repay me from the first available credit on receipt of this note.' When they feel ill and in danger of dying, they have these registers chopped into pieces and swallow them, because they think that, if they were not digested in this way, God would not be able to read them."

This conversation did not prevent us from carrying on our way – that is, my carrier on all fours underneath me, and myself riding along on his back. I will not go into any more detail about the adventures that delayed us en route: suffice it to say that we finally arrived at the King's place of residence. I was taken straight to the palace. The nobles received me with more moderate exclamations of surprise than the ordinary people had done when I passed through their streets. Nonetheless, they reached the same conclusion – namely that I was doubtless the female of the Queen's pet animal. My guide interpreted their words thus, and yet it was something of a riddle for him too, as he did not know what the Queen's pet animal might be; but we were soon enlightened, since the King, a short time afterwards, ordered it to be brought over. Half an hour later I saw, entering in the midst of a troop of monkeys wearing ruffs and breeches, a little man of much the same shape and size as myself, walking on two legs like me; as soon as he set eyes on me, he greeted me with a *criado de nuestra mercede*.* I replied to his bow in much the same terms. But alas, no sooner had they seen us speaking together than they all believed their assumption was right, and the outcome of this turn of events was merely that the spectator most inclined to favour us stoutly asserted that our conversation was a muffled grunting which our joy at being reunited made us utter by a natural instinct.

This little man told me that he was a European, a native of Old Castile, and that he had found a means of getting birds to transport him to the world of the moon in which we were. He had fallen into the hands of the Queen, who had taken him for a monkey, because it so happens that in that country they dress monkeys in Spanish fashion – and thus, finding him on his arrival dressed in that guise, she had been quite convinced that he was of that species.

"The only conclusion to be drawn," I replied, "is that after trying all sorts of clothes on the monkeys, they decided that there were none more ridiculous, and for that reason they dress them in this way, and keep these animals only for amusement."

"That," he replied, "is an injustice to the dignity of our nation; if the universe produces men, it is only so that they may serve us Spaniards as slaves: for us, all that nature brings forth can only be a subject of laughter."

He then bade me to tell him how I had ventured to rise up to the moon with the machine I had mentioned; I replied that it was because he had already used the birds on which I had been hoping to travel. He smiled at this mocking reply and about a quarter of an hour later the King ordered the keepers of the monkeys to take us away, with express orders to ensure that the Spaniard and I slept together, so that we might multiply our species in his kingdom.

The monarch's will was carried out at every point, and I was highly pleased, since this gave me the pleasure of having someone to converse with during the solitude of my brutification. One day, my male (for I was seen as the female) told me that what had really obliged him to travel over the face of the earth and finally to abandon it for the moon was that he had not been able to find a single country where imagination itself was at liberty.

"You see," he told me, "unless you wear a square bonnet, a hood or a surplice,* whatever you say, however eloquent, will – if it goes against the principles of those learned gentlemen of the cloth – mark you down as an idiot, a madman or an atheist. In my country they wanted to haul me up before the Inquisition because I told those obstinate pedants to their beards that nature contains a vacuum and that I knew of no substance in the world heavier than any other."

I asked him what evidence there was to support an opinion that was so little accepted.

"If you're ever going to understand it," he replied, "you need to imagine that there is only one element – even though we see water, air and fire separately, we never find them so perfectly pure that they are completely unmixed with each other. When you look at fire, for example, it isn't really fire – it's nothing but highly attenuated air; air is simply highly dilated water; water is nothing but melted earth; and earth itself is nothing other than highly condensed water. So if you examine matter closely, you'll find that there is only one sort that, like an excellent actress, plays every sort of role in our world, in every sort of costume. Otherwise we would have to accept that there are as many elements as there are sorts of body, and if you then ask me why it is that fire burns and water chills, seeing that it is only one and the same matter, my answer is that this matter acts by sympathy, following the disposition in which it finds itself at the time of action. Fire, which is nothing other than earth even more attenuated than when it constitutes air, tries to change everything it meets into earth, by sympathy. Thus the heat of coal, as the most subtle fire and the most able to penetrate a body, slips between the pores of our mass, and initially makes us dilate, because it is a new matter filling us, and makes us break out into a sweat; this sweat, attenuated by the fire, is converted into steam and becomes air; this air, melted even more by the heat of the antiperistasis,* or the neighbouring stars, is called fire, and earth – when abandoned by the cold and the damp that had been binding together the parts of our body – falls to dust. Water, however, although it differs from the matter of fire only in being more condensed, does not burn us because, being condensed, it longs by sympathy to condense in turn the bodies that it meets, and the cold that you feel is nothing other than the effect of our flesh curling round on itself by the proximity of earth or water constraining it to resemble them. Thus it is that people suffering from dropsy and filled with water change into water all the nourishment that they ingest; thus it is that bilious people change into bile all the blood created by their livers. So, supposing that there is only one single element, it is indubitable that all bodies, each according to its quantity, incline equally to the centre of the earth.

"But you will ask me why it is then that gold, iron, metals, earth and wood descend towards that centre more quickly than a sponge, if not because the sponge is full of air, which tends naturally to rise? That is not at all the reason. Let me explain: although a rock falls more rapidly than a feather, both of them have the same inclination for this journey, but if, for example, a cannonball found that there was a hole in the earth, it would plunge more quickly to its heart than a wind-filled bladder, and the reason is that this mass of metal is a great deal of earth, tamped together into a narrow area, and this wind is a very small amount of earth spread out through a large volume of space; for all the parts of the matter dwelling in this iron, embraced by each other as they are, increase their strength by their unity. Being packed together, they eventually find themselves as a multitude battling against a very small quantity, seeing that the volume of air equal to a cannonball is not equal to it in mass. So the air, giving way before the weight of people who are more numerous than it is, and in just as much haste, it allows itself to be broken apart so as to let them through.

"I won't go into a whole string of arguments to prove this, but merely ask you how on earth you imagine that a pike, a rapier or a dagger can wound us unless it is because the steel is made of matter in which each part is closer to (and more deeply embedded in) every other part than is the case in your flesh, whose pores and soft, yielding nature show that it contains but a small amount of earth spread over a large area. And the point of the iron that pierces us, being of an almost incalculable quantity of matter as against such a small amount of flesh, forces it to yield to the stronger, just as a squadron of cavalry packed closely together can penetrate an entire line of battle which is widely extended. Why else is a red-hot steel ingot hotter than a block of burning wood, if not that there is more fire in the small volume of the ingot attached to every part of that piece of metal than in the log of wood which, being very spongy, contains a great deal of empty space? Empty space or vacuum, being merely a privation of being, cannot assume the shape of fire. But, you will object, you are presupposing the existence of the vacuum as if you had proved it, and that is just where we disagree! Well, I'll now prove it to you, and even though this difficulty is the sister of the Gordian knot, my arms are strong enough to be its Alexander.*

"So then, let them answer – those common blockheads who believe they are men only because some man of learning has told them so! Supposing there is only one kind of matter, as I believe I have adequately proved, how is it that this matter can expand and contract as its appetite wills? How is it that a clod of earth can condense itself until it becomes a pebble? Are the parts of this pebble inserted into each other so that, where one little grain of sand is placed, there, at the very same point, another grain of sand is lodged? No, that is quite impossible, even according to their argument, since bodies cannot penetrate each other, but this matter must have drawn together and, so to speak, grown smaller as it filled the empty space it occupied.

"Can we conclude that this is only possible if there is a vacuum in the world and that we are partly composed of nothing? Well… why not? Is not the entire world surrounded by nothing? Since you're prepared to grant me as much, you have to confess that it is just as easy for the world to have nothing inside it as outside it.

"I can see what you're going to ask me: why is it that water, frozen and congealed in a vessel, makes it burst, if not to prevent a vacuum forming? My answer is that this happens only because the air on top will, just as much as earth and water, tend to the centre of the earth. And if it encounters a vacant hostelry on the direct route to this country, it will take up residence there; if it finds the pores of this vessel (in other words the paths that lead to this chamber of emptiness) too narrow, too long and too twisted, it will break it, at the behest of its impatience to arrive more quickly at its destination.

"But I will not waste time replying to all their objections; I will simply make so bold as to say that if there were no vacuum, there would be no movement – otherwise we have to accept that bodies can penetrate each other, for it will be too ridiculous to believe that, when a fly pushes away a small volume of air with its wing, this volume in turn will force away another one, and this one yet another one, and that the tiny movement of the little toe of a flea can make air gather together on the other side of the world. When they run out of arguments, they resort to rarefaction; but how on earth, when a body is rarefied, can a particle of the mass draw away from another particle without leaving an empty space? Would not these two recently separated bodies need to have been simultaneously in the same place as the latter, so that all three of them interpenetrated? Now I expect you'll ask me why it is that we make water rise against its inclination through a pipe, a syringe or a pump: my answer is that the water is forced to rise, and that it is not the fear it has of a vacuum that obliges it to deviate from its path but that, being joined with the air, in an imperceptible nuance, it rises when one raises the air that holds it in its embrace.

"This cannot be all that difficult for anyone to understand who knows the perfect circle and delicate chain of the elements, for if you pay close attention to the mud created by the marriage of earth and water, you will find that it is no longer earth, or water, but rather a power broker between these two enemies; likewise water and air together send to each other a mist that bends to the humours of both in order to bring about peace between them, and the air is reconciled with the fire by means of a mediating exhalation that unites them."

I think he wanted to go on talking, but just then they brought in our food, and, because we were hungry, I closed my ears and he closed his mouth so we could open our stomachs.*

I remember that on another occasion, as we were philosophizing – since neither of us were particularly inclined to make conversation about vulgar and frivolous things – he said:

"I am really sorry to see a mind of the stamp of yours infected by the errors of the mob. Let me tell you that, in spite of the pedantry of Aristotle with which all the classrooms in your France resound these days, everything is contained in everything else: in other words, inside water, for example, there is fire; inside fire, water; inside air, earth; and inside earth, air. Although this opinion makes the pedants raise their eyebrows, it is easier to prove it than to persuade people it is true. My first question to them is this: whether water engenders fish. When they deny it, I will command them to dig a ditch, fill it with liquid from a pitcher (they can strain it through a sieve if they want to, to counter the objections of the blind); then, if after a while they find no fish in it, I will be quite prepared to drink all the water they poured into it; but if they do find fish there, and I have no doubt they will, this is convincing proof that there is salt and fire in it. Consequently, finding water in fire is not a particularly difficult enterprise. Let them choose even fire at its most detached from matter, such as comets: they will still always find a great quantity of water in them. After all, if the oily humour from which they are formed, reduced to sulphur by the heat of the antiperistasis that makes them glow, did not find an obstacle to its violence in the moist coldness that tempers and combats it, that humour would be suddenly consumed like a flash of lightning. And that there is air in earth they will not deny – or if they do so, they cannot have heard of the terrible tremors by which the mountains of Sicily have so often been shaken. Apart from that, the earth is completely porous, as we can see, even down to the grains of sand that compose it. And yet nobody has ever said that those hollows were filled with a vacuum: so there can be no objection to the air making its dwelling place there. I now have only to prove that in air there is earth, but I can hardly be bothered to do so, since you are convinced of the fact whenever you see, beating down on your heads, those legions of atoms so numerous that they stifle all arithmetic.

"But let us pass from simple bodies to compound bodies: they will provide me with much more evidence that all things are in all things; not that they change into one another, as your

Peripatetics* chirrup – I will maintain to their faces that the principles mingle, separate and mingle again in such a way that what was once made water by the wise Creator of the world will always be water; nor do I presuppose, as they do, any maxim that I cannot prove.

"So take, I beg you, a log, or some other combustible matter, and set fire to it: they for their part will say, when it is alight, that what was wood has become fire. But that is just what I deny, and there is no more fire, now that it is all in flames, than there was before a match was set to it; but the fire that was hidden in the log and which the cold and damp prevented from spreading out and acting has now been given assistance from elsewhere, has rallied its strength against the phlegm stifling it, and has seized the field previously occupied by its enemy; thus it manifests itself without obstacles, and triumphs over its jailer. Do you not see how the water escapes from both ends of the log, still hot and steaming from the battle it has just fought? This flame that you see over it is the most subtle fire, that which is most detached from matter, and thus that which is most ready to return to its native abode. However, it forms a pyramid-shaped unit up to a certain height so as to drive its way through the thick humidity of the air resisting it, but since, as it rises, it gradually disengages itself from the violent company of its hosts, it then bursts out into the open as it no longer encounters anything inimical to its passage, and this negligence is, as often as not, the cause of a second imprisonment, for, as this fire makes its separate way, it will sometimes lose itself in a cloud. If other fires in sufficient number are present to resist the vapour, they will join together, rumble, thunder, lighten – and the death of innocent beings is frequently the effect of the turbulent anger of dead things. If the fire finds itself entangled in the importunate crude matter of the middle region, and is not strong enough to defend itself, it abandons itself to the discretion of the cloud, which, forced by its weight to fall back to earth, takes its prisoner with it, and this unhappy prisoner, enclosed in a drop of water, will

47

perhaps find itself at the foot of an oak tree, whose animal fire will invite this poor stray creature to lodge with it. And in this way we see it reassuming the same condition from which it had started out a few days previously.

"But let us examine the fortune of the other elements of which this log was composed. The air withdraws to its quarter, albeit still mingled with vapours, because the fire, filled with anger, has brusquely driven them pell-mell away. So it serves as a balloon for the winds, provides the animals with breath, fills the vacuum made by nature, and possibly, having wrapped itself in a drop of dew, it will even be sipped and digested by the thirsty leaves of the same tree to which our fire has withdrawn. The water that the flame had driven from this throne, lifted by the heat to the birthplace of meteors, will fall down in the form of rain onto our oak just as soon as onto any other, and the earth, turned to ashes, cured of its sterility by the nourishing heat of the dunghill onto which it has been thrown, by the vegetative salt of various neighbouring plants, and by the fertilizing water of the rivers, will perhaps find itself near this oak which, by the heat of its seed, will attract it and make it a part of its whole.

"In this way, we see these four elements returning to the same condition from which they had set out a few days previously. In this way, there is in a man everything needed to make up a tree; in this way, there is in a tree everything needed to make up a man. Finally, in this way, all things can be found in all things, but we lack a Prometheus to extract them."

These, more or less, were the topics with which we beguiled the time, and truly, this little Spaniard was an ingenious fellow. Our conversations could take place only at night-time, because from six o'clock in the morning until the evening the great throng of people that came to stare at us in our lodgings would have distracted us; some threw stones at us, others nuts, others clumps of grass. The King's animals were the talk of the town.

We were fed every day at regular times, and the King and the Queen themselves took rather frequent pleasure in feeling my belly to find out whether I was swelling out, for they were burning with an extraordinary desire to breed more of these small animals. I do not know whether it was because I had paid more attention than my male to the faces they pulled and the tone of voice they spoke in, but in any case I learnt to understand their language and to speak it just a little. Immediately the news ran the length and breadth of the kingdom that two wild men had been found, smaller than others because of the poor nourishment that solitude had provided us with; because of a defect in our father's seed (they said), our forelegs were not strong enough for us to lean on.

This belief started to spread, and would have taken root, were it not for the priests of the country who opposed it, saying that it was a dreadful impiety to believe that not only animals but monsters too could belong to the same species as them.

"It would be much more plausible," the less impassioned of them added, "if our domestic animals participated in the privilege of humanity, and thus immortality, because they are at least born in our country – they are not some monstrous creature that claims to have been born Heaven knows where on the moon; and then, just look at the difference between them and us! We, at least, walk on all fours, because God did not wish to entrust such a precious thing to a less secure posture; he was afraid that some mishap might happen to man; that is why he himself took the trouble to set him on four pillars, so that he would not fall; but he disdained to become involved with the construction of these two brutes, and abandoned them to the whim of nature, which – unperturbed by the idea that such an insignificant thing might be destroyed – propped him up on just two feet.

"Even the birds," they said, "have not been treated so badly as these beasts, since they have at least been given feathers to make up for the weakness of their feet, and to allow them to fly into the air when we shoo them away from our abodes; whereas nature, by depriving these monsters of two of their feet, has made them unable to escape our justice.

"And just look at the way their heads are turned up towards the heavens! God has caused them to lack everything they need, and thus placed them in this situation – for this supplicant posture shows that they are gazing heavenwards to complain to the one who created them, asking Him for permission to make do with our leftovers. We, however, have our heads lowered so that we can contemplate the good things of which we are the lords, so that there is nothing in heaven that we in our happy condition need envy."

Every day in my lodgings I heard the priests spinning these or similar fairy tales; they eventually managed to bridle people's ideas and opinions on this matter to such an extent that it was decreed I would be deemed to be, at best, a plucked parrot; they preached to the converted that, like any other bird, I had only two feet. So I was put in a cage on the express orders of the Upper Council.

Here, every day, the Queen's fowler took the trouble to come and whistle the language to me as we do here to starlings, and indeed I was happy that I did not go short of food in my coop. In the mean time, from the idiotic remarks with which the spectators assailed my ears, I learnt to speak like them. Once I had mastered their tongue enough to express most of my ideas, I could really tell them a tale or two. Already, whenever people gathered together, the conversation dwelt exclusively on the neatness of my witty sallies, and the esteem in which my intelligence was held rose so high that the clergy were obliged to have a decree published in which it was forbidden to believe that I was endowed with reason, with the most express command, to all persons of whatever quality and condition they might be, that, however much wit I might show, they should assume it was instinct alone that impelled me.

However, the definition of what I was divided the city into two factions. The party that supported me grew every day. Finally, in spite of the anathema and excommunication issued by the prophets, who were attempting to intimidate the people, those in my party demanded an assembly of the states to resolve this prickly point in religion. They took a long time deciding who would be on the jury, but those called in to arbitrate quietened all animosity by ensuring that the numbers on both sides would be equal. I was ceremonially brought into the law court, where I was treated severely by the examiners. Among other things, they interrogated me on philosophy: in all good faith I set out the things I had formerly been taught by my tutor, but they found little difficulty in refuting me, supporting their arguments with many reasons that were indeed most convincing. When I saw that I was completely beaten, I quoted as a last resort the principles of Aristotle, which were of no more use to me than those sophisms, for they needed but a few words to show me that they were false. Aristotle, they told me, fitted his principles to his philosophy instead of fitting his philosophy to his principles. Furthermore, he should at least have proved that those principles were more reasonable than those of the other sects, which he was unable to do. "That is why the good chap must not be vexed with us if we bid him farewell," they added.

Finally, seeing that I kept babbling on that they were no wiser than Aristotle and that I had been forbidden to argue against those who denied his principles, they unanimously concluded that I was not a man but possibly some kind of ostrich, since like that creature I bore my head erect. As a result the fowler was ordered to put me back in my cage. Here I spent my time pleasantly enough, since now that I was able to speak the language correctly, the whole Court enjoyed coming and listening to me chatter. The Queen's daughters, among others, were always stuffing some little tit-bit into my basket; and the kindest of them all had started to feel really quite friendly towards me. She was quite ecstatic when, one time we were alone together, I revealed to her the mysteries of our religion, especially when I told her of our church bells and our relics – indeed, she protested, with tears in her eyes, that if ever I found myself able to fly back to our world, she would be delighted to come with me.

One day, I woke up very early with a start, and saw her drumming her fingers against the bars of my cage.

"I have great news!" she said to me. "Yesterday the Council decided to declare war on the great King ▰▰. I hope that in the hustle and bustle of the preparations, while our monarch and his subjects are far away, an opportunity can be found to set you free."

"What! War?" I broke in. "Do quarrels arise between the princes of this world just as in our world? Ah! Please tell me how they fight their wars."

"The referees," she replied, "are elected by the two parties, and they designate the time granted for arming and marching, the number of combatants and the day and place of the battle, all with such a precise sense of equity that there is not a single man more in one army than in the other. The maimed soldiers on each side are all enrolled in a particular company, and when the fighting begins, the field officers take care to set them against the maimed soldiers on the other side. Likewise, giants square up to colossi; fencers fight against the nimble; the valiant against the brave; the weak against the feeble; the unwell against the sick; the robust against the strong – and if anyone takes it into his head to strike another man than his designated enemy, unless he can justify himself by pleading that it was a mistake, he is condemned as a coward. After the battle they count the wounded, the dead and the prisoners; no one is ever seen to run away. If losses are equal on both sides, they draw straws to decide who can claim the victory.

"But even though the one king has defeated his enemy fairly and squarely, nothing has yet been achieved, since there are other, much less numerous armies of scholars and men of wit, and on their disputes the real triumph or servitude of states entirely depends.

"One scholar opposes another scholar, one man of wit another man of wit, one wise man another wise man. And the triumph won by a state in this way counts for three victories won by open force. When a nation is proclaimed victorious, they break up the gathering and the victorious people chooses as its king either the king of its enemies or its own."

I could not help laughing at this fastidious way of fighting battles, and as an example of a much stronger policy I cited the customs of our Europe, where the monarch takes care not to neglect any advantage that will ensure victory. She replied to me in these terms:

"Tell me – do your princes justify their resort to weapons by simply claiming that might is right?"

"No," I replied. "They justify themselves by claiming that their cause is just."

"So why," she continued, "do they not choose referees who are above suspicion to negotiate a peace? And if it so happens that there is as much right on one side as on the other, let them stay the way they were, or let them play a hand of piquet for the city or province over which they are quarrelling. For while they are causing the heads of four million men all better than they are to be smashed in on their behalf, they are sitting in their little rooms swapping jokes about the details of the massacre of those poor fools. But I'm wrong to criticize the valour of your brave subjects in this way: they do well to die for their country; it is a matter of some importance – whether one is the vassal of a king who wears a ruff or one who wears a turned-down collar."

"But what about you?" I replied. "Why do you make your way of fighting so very complicated? Isn't it enough for the armies to have equal numbers of men?"

"You have little judgement," she replied. "Would you, by your faith, think you had beaten on the field your enemy in single combat, in a fair fight, if you were wearing mail and he were not? Or if he had merely a dagger, and you a rapier? Or if he had only one arm and you had two?

"Yet for all the equality that you so highly recommend for your gladiators, they are never evenly matched when they fight, for the one will be tall, and the other short; the one will be nimble and the other will never have handled a sword; the one will be robust and the other weak. And even if these disproportions were evened out so that they were equally tall, equally nimble and equally strong as each other, they would still not be the same, for one of the two will perhaps have more courage than the other; the more brutal man will not pay heed to his danger, will be bilious in temperament and will have more blood in him and a more determined heart, together with all those qualities that make up courage – and are these not, just as much as the sword, a weapon which his enemy is lacking? He will contrive to charge headlong at his opponent, to terrify him and to deprive of life that poor man who had seen the danger in advance, whose vital heat was stifled in phlegm and whose heart was too large to gather the spirits necessary for dissipating the ice that is called poltroonery. And so you praise that man for having killed his enemy when the first had the advantage, and, in praising his boldness, you are praising him for a sin against nature, since boldness will tend to destroy him.

"Let me tell you that, a few years ago, a remonstrance was made to the Council of War requesting that a more circumspect and conscientious ruling be applied to combat, for the philosopher giving this advice spoke in these terms:

"'You imagine, gentlemen, that you have evened out the advantages of the two enemies when you have chosen them both to be hardy, both tall, both nimble and both filled with courage, but that is still not enough since, after all, the victor must win by skill, strength or fortune. If it is by skill, he doubtless struck his adversary in a place where he was not expecting it, or more swiftly than had seemed likely; or, feigning to attack him on one side, he thrust at him from the other. This is all a matter of finesse, deception, treachery. And finesse, deception and treachery should not be any ground for esteeming a man truly noble.

If he has conquered by strength, will you deem that his enemy has been vanquished because he has been overwhelmed by force? No, surely not – no more than you will say that a man has lost the victory even though he has been crushed by the collapse of a mountain – after all, there is no possibility of him winning the victory in *this* case. In the same way, the man in question was not overcome because he was not in a position to be able to resist the violent attacks of his enemy. If it was by chance that he cut down his enemy, it is Fortune and not he that should be crowned: he contributed nothing to it, and indeed a beaten man should no more be criticized than a dice-player who has thrown a seventeen and sees his opponent throwing an eighteen.'

"Everyone admitted that he was right, but that it was impossible, given the human condition, to remedy the situation, and that it was better to put up with a small inconvenience than to lay oneself open to a thousand worse difficulties."

On that occasion she said no more to me, as she was afraid she might be found alone with me at such an early hour of the day. Not that in that country unchastity is a crime; on the contrary, apart from convicted criminals, every man has power over every woman, and in the same way a woman can take a man to court if he refuses her favours. But she did not dare to frequent me openly, she told me, because the priests had declared at their last sacrifice that it was mainly women who spread the rumour that I was a man, as a pretext to cover the execrable desire with which they burned to conjoin with animals, and shamelessly to commit sins against nature with me. This was the reason why I went for so long without seeing her or anyone else of her sex.

Meanwhile, someone must have stirred up the debate about the definition of my being, for as I was now starting to be resigned to dying in my cage, I was given another hearing. I was interrogated, in the presence of many courtiers, on some point in physics, and my replies, I believe, were deemed unsatisfactory, for, in far from magisterial tones, the man presiding set out to me at great length his opinions on the structure of the world. They struck me as ingenious, and if he had not gone right back to its origin, maintaining that it was eternal, I would have found his philosophy much more reasonable than ours. But as soon as I heard him maintaining a flimsy opinion, so contrary to what faith teaches us, I asked him what he would say in reply to the authority of Moses, the great patriarch who had said quite clearly that God had created the world in six days. That ignoramus merely laughed instead of answering my question. So I was obliged to tell him that, if such was his opinion, I was starting to believe that their world was merely a moon.

"But you can see land here," they all replied, "and forests, rivers and seas: what could they all be if not earth?"

"Never mind that!" I retorted. "Aristotle assures us that it is merely the moon; and if you had said the contrary in the classes in which I studied, you would have been hissed."

At this, there was a great roar of laughter. You need not ask whether this was a result of their ignorance. I was taken back into my cage.

However, the priests were told that I had dared to say that the moon was a world from which I came, and their world merely a moon. They felt this provided them with a perfectly justified pretext for having me condemned to death by water – this is their means of exterminating atheists. They all went in a body to lodge a complaint with the King, and he promised them justice; it was ordered that I should once again be put in the dock.

So I was uncaged for the third time; the Great Pontiff took the floor and spoke against me. I do not remember his harangue because I was too terrified to hear the utterances of his voice without shivering in dread, and also because in his declamations he was using an instrument whose noise deafened me: this was a trumpet that he had chosen deliberately so that the violence of its martial tone would stir up their spirits to seek my death and, by arousing their passions, prevent reason from performing its office, as happens in our armies, where the greater din of trumpets and drums prevent a soldier from reflecting on the importance of his life.

When he had spoken, I rose to defend my cause, but I was relieved of the need to do so by something that happened. I will tell you about it. I had just opened my mouth when a man who had forced his way through the crowd only with great difficulty came and fell before the King's seat and dragged himself about on his back for a long time. This behaviour came as no surprise to me, for I had long known that this was the posture they assumed when they wished to make a speech in public. So I merely pocketed my speech; this is the speech that we had from him:

"Just men, hear me! You cannot possibly condemn this man, monkey or parrot for saying that the moon was a world from which he came, for he is a man, even if he did not come from the moon, and all men are free – so is he not free to imagine whatever he likes? Good Heavens! Can you force him to see things exactly the same way that you do? You can indeed force him to say that he believes the moon is not a world, but he will still not really believe it, for in order to believe something, it is necessary that one's imagination be presented with certain possibilities greater than the mere yes or no of the thing. Thus, unless you provide him with this likelihood, or unless it spontaneously offers itself to his mind, he will indeed tell you that he believes it: but he won't.

"Now I need to prove to you that he must not be condemned if you place him in the category of animals.

"Suppose that he is an animal that reasons, what reason do you yourselves have for accusing him of sinning against reason? He has said that the moon is a world; now a brute beast acts only through an instinct of Nature, so it is Nature that says so, and not he himself. So to believe that Nature in her wisdom, who made both the moon and this world, does not herself know what it is and that the rest of you, whose knowledge is entirely derived from her, know it with any more certainty, would be perfectly ridiculous. But even if passion led you to renounce your first principles, so that you supposed that nature did not guide the brute beasts, you should at least blush at the disquiet that the mere caperings of one such beast have caused you. Truly, gentlemen, if you were to meet a man of mature years who is keeping an anthill under surveillance, either so that he could cuff an ant that had tripped over its colleague, or so that he could send to jail an ant who had stolen a grain of wheat from its neighbour, or bring a lawsuit against another that had abandoned its eggs, wouldn't you consider that he was crazy to waste his time on subjects so far beneath him, and to try to make creatures submit to reason when they are deprived of it? Venerable pontiffs, what then will you call the interest that you are taking in the caperings of this little animal? Men of justice, I rest my case."

As soon as he had finished, a loud music of applause echoed throughout the hall, and when all opinions had been debated for a good quarter of an hour, this is what the King decided. From now on I would be deemed to be a man, as such set free, and the punishment of being drowned would be commuted into making ignominious amends (for in that country there is no such thing as honourable amends); these amends would consist of myself publicly retracting my teaching that the moon was a world, because of the scandal that the novelty of this opinion might have caused in the souls of the weaker sort.

As soon as the sentence had been pronounced, I was taken out of the palace, and to show off my ignominy I was dressed quite magnificently and borne on the platform of a superb chariot, and as I was pulled along by four princes who had been yoked to the chariot, this is what they forced me to utter at every crossroad in the city:

"People, I declare to you that this moon here is not a moon, but a world; and that the world over there is not a world, but a moon. Such is the belief that the priests deem you should hold."

After I had cried out the same thing on the five great squares of the city, I noticed my lawyer holding out his hand to me, to help me get down. I was most astonished to realize on closer inspection that he was my old demon. We spent a full hour hugging one another.

"And now," he told me, "you must come to my place, as if you returned to the Court after making ignominious amends, you would not be made to feel very welcome. In addition, I have to tell you that you would still be with the monkeys, as would the Spaniard, your companion, if I had not gone round telling everybody of the strength and vigour of your mind, and solicited the protection of the nobles in your favour, against the prophets."

I was still thanking him as he arrived at his home and went in; he spent the time until our meal was served informing me of all the wheels he had set turning in order to force the priests – in spite of the most specious scruples with which they had cajoled the minds of the people – to allow him to give me a hearing. We were sitting in front of a roaring fire because the season was cold, and he was (I think) about to continue telling me what he had been doing all the time I had not seen him, when we were informed that dinner was ready.

"I have invited two professors from the Academy of the city to come and eat with us this evening," he went on. "I will lead them round to the subject of the philosophy that they teach in this world. You will also have a chance to see my host's son. He is a young man as intelligent as any I have ever met, and might be a second Socrates if he could bring order into his luminous ideas and not allow his vicious way of living to stifle the graces with which God continually infuses him, and if he would cease to make such an extravagant show of impiety. I have taken up lodgings here to spy out every opportunity of instructing him."

He paused, as if to give me in turn an opportunity to speak; then he signalled that I should be divested of the shameful robes in which I was still sitting resplendent.

The two professors for whom we were waiting came in almost immediately, and there were four of us together in the little dining room where we also found the boy whom he had mentioned, already eating. They bowed most deeply to him, and treated him with as much profound respect as a slave does his lord. I asked my demon why, and he replied that it was because of his age, since in that world old people pay every sort of honour and deference to the young; indeed, fathers there obey their children as soon as the Senate of philosophers decrees that they have reached the age of reason.

"Are you surprised," he continued, "at a custom so completely different from that of your own country? And yet it is in no way repugnant to right reason; in all good conscience, tell me, when a young, ardent man has enough strength to imagine, judge and execute, is he not more capable of governing a family than an infirm sexagenarian? That poor dodderer whose imagination has been frozen by the snows of sixty winters bases his behaviour on events that just happened to turn out well – and yet it is fortune that ensured this, against every rule and the whole economy of human prudence. As for judgement, he has just as little of that, even though the ordinary folk in your world consider judgement to be a prerogative of old age. To relieve them of this illusion they ought to realize that what in an old man we call prudence is merely a panic-stricken apprehension, a mad and obsessive fear of embarking on any enterprise at all. Thus, my son, when he has not dared to face a danger in which a young man met his doom, it is not because he was able to foresee the catastrophe, but because he did not have enough fire to light that noble enthusiasm that makes us bold to act – and this young man's audacity was like a pledge of the success of his plans, because that ardour that means he can carry out quickly and easily what he undertakes was the very same that had launched him on his enterprise. As for putting one's plans into practice, I would be doing your intelligence a disservice if I endeavoured to convince you by proof. You know already that youth alone is the proper time for action, and if you are not altogether convinced, then tell me, please: when you respect a brave man, is it not because he can avenge you for what your enemies or oppressors have done to you? So why do you still respect him, if not out of habit alone, when a battalion of seventy Januarys has frozen his blood and killed off with its icy grip all the noble enthusiasm for justice that inflames young people? When you defer to a strong man, is it not so that he may be obliged to you for a victory which you could never have won? So why should you submit to him when sloth has eroded his muscles, weakened his arteries, evaporated his spirits and sucked the marrow out of his bones? If you adore a woman, is it not because of her beauty? So why should you continue with your genuflections once old age has turned her into a spectre, menacing living people with death? And finally, when you honour an intelligent man, it is because through the vivacity of his genius he can cut straight through some complex business and resolve it, because he can delight by his eloquence an assembly of the highest distinction, and absorb the sciences in a single thought, so that every noble soul will be filled with a vehement desire to resemble him. And yet you continue to pay homage to him when his worn-out organs make him heavy-headed and feeble of mind and when in company his silence makes him resemble the statue of a household deity rather than a man capable of reason.

"You may conclude from all this, my son, that it is better for young men rather than old men to govern families. Of course, it would be silly of you to think that Hercules, Achilles, Epaminondas, Alexander and Caesar, who all died before they reached forty,* were men to whom only an ordinary respect was due, and that some old dotard should, simply because the sun has ripened his harvest ninety times over, be worshipped by you with incense.

"But, you will say, all the laws of our world insist on stating over and over again how much respect is owed to old men. That is true: but it is also true that all those who have introduced such laws have been old men who feared that the younger might justifiably dispossess them of the authority they had extorted, and they have acted like the legislators of false religions, making a mystery of what they were unable to prove.

"Yes, you will say: but this old man is my father, and Heaven promises me a long life if I honour him. If, my son, your father does not order you to do anything that goes against the inspirations of the Highest, I grant that you are right; otherwise, trample underfoot the belly of the father who begot you, and stamp on the breast of the mother who conceived you, for I do not find it at all likely that the cowardly respect that wicked parents have dragged out of you, in your weakness, can be so agreeable to Heaven that it will spin out a long life for you. What? You raise your hat to tickle and nourish the pride of your father – but will this lance, an abscess that you have in your side, will it repair your over-moist radical, will it cure a rapier wound through your stomach, will it disperse a stone in your bladder? If so, the doctors are completely wrong: instead of the infernal potions with which they plague men's lives, they should prescribe for smallpox three low bows on an empty stomach, four 'humble thanks' after dinner and twelve doses of 'good evening, Father, good evening, Mother' before the patient goes to bed. You will reply that, without your father, you would not exist; that is true, but in turn he himself would never have existed without your grandfather, your grandfather without your great-grandfather, and that without you, your father would have no grandsons. When Nature brought him forth, it was on condition that he should give back what she had lent him; so when he begot you, he gave you nothing, he was simply paying a debt! Indeed, I would really like to know whether your parents were even thinking of you when they made you. Alas, not at all! And yet you believe yourself obliged to them for a present they gave you without even thinking of it. What! Because your father was such a lecher that he could not resist the lovely eyes of some loose woman that he haggled over to assuage his passion, and you were the masonry that arose from their pawings, you revere that lustful fellow as if he were one of the seven sages of Greece! What! Because that other miser purchased the wealthy endowment of his wife by giving her a child in return, should that child speak to him only on his knees? In that way your father was quite right to be lascivious and that other man to be niggardly, because otherwise neither you nor he would ever have existed – but I would very much like to know whether, even if he had been certain that his pistol shot would misfire, he would still not have pulled the trigger. Good God! What fables they foist on the ordinary folk in your world.

"My son, it is only your body that you take from your mortal architect; your soul comes from the heavens, and could just as well have sheathed itself in some other scabbard. Your father could quite possibly have been born your son, just as you were born his son. How do you even know that he has not perhaps prevented you from inheriting a royal diadem? Perhaps your spirit had come down from heaven with the intention of dwelling in the body of the King of the Romans, in the womb of the Empress; on its way it just happened to encounter your embryo; to shorten its trip, it took up lodgings there. No, no, God would never have struck you off the list of plans he had made for mankind, even if your father had died while still a small boy. But who knows but you might not today be the work of some valiant captain, who would have made you an associate of his glory and enabled you to share in his fortune? So perhaps you owe no more to your father for the life he has given you than you would have done to the pirate who put you in chains – he too would at least feed you. One might even suppose that he had begotten you to be a king; a present loses its merit when it is made without any choice on the part of the person receiving it. Caesar was killed, and so was Cassius; however, Cassius remains under the obligation of the slave from whom he begged for death, whereas Caesar is in no debt to his murderers, who forced death upon him.* Did your father consult your desires when he took your mother in his arms? Or did he ask you whether you would like to see life in this century, rather than waiting for another one? Whether you would be content with being the son of a fool, or whether you yearned to be the offspring of a fine fellow? Alas! You were the only person involved, and yet you were the only person whose opinion was not asked! After all, perhaps, if you had been enfolded somewhere other than in the womb of Nature's ideas, and if your birth had been of your choosing, you would have said to Fate: 'My dear lady, take up the spindle of somebody else; I have been suspended in nothingness for a very long time, and I far prefer remaining in non-being for another hundred years rather than coming into being today and then repenting of it tomorrow.' Still, this is the lot you had to endure; you could wail as much as you liked, pleading to return to the long dark house from which you had been plucked; everyone simply pretended to believe that you were asking to suckle.

"These, my son, are pretty much the reasons behind the respect that fathers pay their children; I know that I have favoured the children's side rather more than justice requires, and that I have spoken on their behalf somewhat against my conscience. But, as I wish to correct the insolent pride with which fathers insult the weakness of their offspring, I have been obliged to behave like those who wish to straighten out the twisted tree, bending it in the opposite direction so that, between two contortions, it returns to its original straightness. So I have restored to the fathers the tyrannical deference that they had usurped, and have taken from them much that belonged to them, so that in future they will be content with their share. I know full well that this apologia of mine has shocked all old men, but they need merely remember that they were sons before being fathers, and that I cannot have failed to speak greatly to their advantage, since they were not found under a gooseberry bush.* But anyway, whatever may happen, even if my enemies engage in battle against my friends, it will turn out for the best for me, since I have served all men, and done a disservice to only half of them."

Thereupon he fell silent, and our host's son began as follows:

"Since you have taken the trouble to instruct me on the origin, history, customs and philosophy of this little man's world, please allow me to add something to what you've said, so that I can prove that children owe nothing to their fathers for their begetting, since their fathers were obliged in all conscience to beget them.

"Even the narrowest philosophy of their world accepts that it is more desirable to die – since in order to die you have to have lived – than never to be at all. Now, since if I do not give being to that nothing, I put it in a worse state than death, and I am more guilty of not producing it than of killing it. You would believe, my little man, that you have committed an unforgivable parricide if you had murdered your son; your crime would indeed be horrendous; and yet it is much more execrable not to give being to a creature that may receive it, for if you deprive a child of the light of life, he at least had the satisfaction of enjoying it for a time. In addition, we know that he is deprived of it for only a few centuries, but those forty poor little nothings, from which you could have made fine soldiers for your King, have been maliciously prevented by you from coming into being, and you leave them to rot away in your loins, exposed to the risk of a fit of apoplexy that will choke you. Let nobody object to my argument by proposing to sing the praises of virginity: that honour is nothing but smoke, since, after all, the respect with which ordinary people revere it amounts – even amongst you and your kind – to no more than a piece of advice, whereas you are commanded not to kill, and to deign to create a son for yourself rather than not bringing him into being at all (thus making him more wretched than a dead man). That is why I am highly surprised, given that chastity in the world from which you come is considered so very preferable to carnal propagation, that God has not caused you to be born from the dews of May like mushrooms, or at least like crocodiles from the thick slime of the earth when it is heated by the sun. And yet he sends eunuchs among you only by accident:

he does not tear the genitals from your monks, your priests or your cardinals. You will tell me that it was nature that gave them those organs; yes, but he is the master of nature, and if he had thought that this part of the body were harmful to their salvation, he would have commanded it to be cut off, as the Jews did the prepuce in the Old Law. But this is quite a ridiculous way of seeing things. Good Heavens, is there any part of your body that is more sacred or more accursed than any other? Why am I committing a sin when I touch myself in my middle parts and not when I touch my ear or my heel? Is it because it tickles? If so, I ought not to purge myself in the basin, since it is really rather enjoyable, and the devout ought not to rise to the contemplation of God, since they enjoy an intense pleasure of the imagination in doing so. I am truly surprised, seeing how much the religion of your country goes against nature and enviously frustrates all the little pleasures of men, that the priests have not made it a crime to scratch yourself, because of the agreeable pain that you feel when you do so; with all that, I've noticed that Nature in her wisdom has made all great personages, both the valiant and the gifted among them, inclined to the delicate pleasures of love – witness Samson, David, Hercules, Caesar, Hannibal and Charlemagne; was it so that they should harvest the organ of this pleasure with a slice of the sickle? Alas! Nature even sought out Diogenes in his tub, skinny, ugly and covered with lice, and forced him to compose, from the breath with which he cooled his carrots, lovesick sighs for Lais.* Nature doubtless behaved in this way for fear there would otherwise be a lack of honest men in the world. We may conclude from this that your father was obliged in all conscience to let you out into the light, and even if he thinks he has greatly indebted you by creating you with a quick tickle of his loins, basically he has merely given you what any common or garden bull gives his calves when he has his fun ten times a day."

"You are wrong," my demon then interrupted, "to try to regulate the wisdom of God. It is true that he has forbidden us to indulge in this pleasure to excess, but how do you know that he has not done so in order that the difficulties we encounter in struggling against this passion will enable us to merit the glory that he is preparing for us? And how do you know that he did not act this way to sharpen our appetites by forbidding this pleasure? And how do you know that he did not foresee that, if young people abandoned themselves to the impetuousness of the flesh, their over-frequent intercourse would weaken their seed and mean the world came to an abrupt end with the grandchildren of the first man? And how do you know that he did not want to prevent the fertility of the earth being insufficient for the needs of so many hungry people? And finally, how do you know that he did not want to impose this prohibition against every appearance of reason so as to give a just reward to those who, also against all appearance of reason, trust in his word?"

This reply did not, I believe, satisfy our small host, since he shook his head two or three times, but the tutor we shared said nothing, since our meal was in a hurry to fly away.

So we stretched out on some very soft mattresses covered with great rugs, where the odours came to seek us out as they had done before at the inn. A young servant took the older of our two philosophers and led him to a small separate room.

"Come back and find us here," my tutor called to him, "as soon as you have eaten."

He promised he would.

The strange idea of eating alone made me curious, and I asked for the reason.

"He does not enjoy," I was told, "the odour of meat, or even of vegetables, unless they died of their own accord, since he believes they are capable of feeling pain."

"I am not particularly surprised," I replied, "that he should abstain from flesh and all things that have enjoyed a sensitive life, for in our world the Pythagoreans, and even a few saintly hermits, have followed the same diet. But not daring, for example, to cut a cabbage for fear of wounding it strikes me as completely laughable."

"And as for me," replied the demon, "I find his opinion quite plausible: after all, tell me – this cabbage you mentioned is surely as much a creature of God as you are? Do not both of you have God and Privation as your father and mother? Has God's intellect not been occupied for all eternity with the birth of the cabbage as much as with yours? Indeed, it seems that he has more necessarily provided for the birth of the vegetable than for that of the reasonable creature, since he has placed the generation of a man at the whim of his father, who could, as his pleasure decreed, either beget him or not, and yet he refused to treat the cabbage with the same severity; instead of placing it in the father's discretion whether or not to engender his son, God, as if more fearful that the race of cabbages might perish than that of men, constrains them to give themselves to each other whether they are willing or not, quite unlike men, who at best can engender in their whole lives only a score or so, while cabbages can produce four hundred thousand of their kind per head. And yet, if we say that God has loved man more than he has loved the cabbage, we are simply tickling ourselves to make ourselves laugh; since he is incapable of passion, he can neither hate nor love anybody, and if he were prone to love, he would feel more affection for the cabbage you are holding, which is unable to disobey him, than for the man who, as he can see already, is bound to offend him. In addition to this, a man cannot be born without crime, being part of the first man who made him guilty, but we know perfectly well that the first cabbage did not offend its Creator in the earthly Paradise.

"Can anyone say that we are made in the image of the Sovereign Being, and that cabbages are not? Even if this is true, we, by sullying our souls where we most resemble him, have effaced this resemblance, since there is nothing more contrary to God than sin. So, if our souls are not his portrait, we do not resemble him any more by our hands, feet, mouths, brows and ears than the cabbage by its leaves, its flowers, its stalk, its heart and its head. Do you really not think that, if this poor plant could speak when it were cut, it would say: 'Man, my dear brother, what have I done to deserve death? I grow only in your gardens, and I am never found in wild places where I could live in safety; I disdained to be the work of any hands other than yours, but no sooner have I left your hands than I fall back into them. I rise from the ground, I blossom, I hold out my arms to you, I offer you my children as seedlings, and the only reward for my courtesy is that you cut my head off!'

"This is the speech the cabbage would make if it could express itself. Ah! Just because it cannot complain, does that mean it is right for us to hurt it in all sorts of ways that it cannot prevent? If I come across some wretched man in chains, can I kill him without committing a crime, just because he cannot defend himself? On the contrary, his weakness would make my action even crueller, and however much that unfortunate creature may be poor and lacking in all our advantages, it does not deserve death. What! Of all the benefits of being, it has only that of vegetable existence – and we rid it even of that! The sin of murdering a man is not so terrible (since one day he will live again) as the sin of cutting a cabbage and depriving it of life, since it has no other life to look forward to. You annihilate the soul of a cabbage if you put it to death, but in killing a man you simply make him change his dwelling place; indeed, I would go further: since God, the common father of all things, cherishes all his creatures equally, it is surely sensible that he should have shared out his benefits equally between us and the plants. It is true that we were born first, but in God's family there is no right of seniority: so if cabbages were not given the inheritance of immortality with us, it is doubtless because they were granted some other advantage to make up for the brevity of their lives – maybe a universal intellect, a perfect knowledge of all things in their courses: and this is perhaps also the reason why that wise Maker did not fashion for them organs similar to ours, organs that produce nothing more than an elementary, feeble and often deceptive reasoning: he gave them instead other organs, more ingeniously shaped, stronger and more numerous, which enable them to indulge in their speculative conversations. Perhaps you will ask me which of their great thoughts they have ever communicated to us? But tell me, have angels ever taught us any more than cabbages have? Since there is no proportion, relation or harmony between the weak and feeble faculties of man and those of such divine creatures, those intellectual cabbages could do all in their power to enlighten us as to the occult causes of all the marvellous things that occur, and we would still lack senses capable of grasping such lofty notions.

"Moses, the greatest of all philosophers (since according to you he drew his understanding of nature from the very source of nature), conveyed this truth when he described the Tree of Knowledge: in the form of this riddle he wanted to teach us that plants exclusively possess the perfect philosophy. So remember, you who of all animals are the most haughty, that even though a cabbage that you cut does not utter a single word, it thinks no less. The poor vegetable does not have any organs enabling it to howl like you; no organs with which to shudder and weep; but it does have organs with which it can complain of the evil you are doing it, and thereby draws down on your heads the vengeance of Heaven. If you ask me how I know that cabbages entertain these fine thoughts, let me ask you how you know that they do *not*, and that a certain cabbage, for instance, may not imitate you, saying, as it closes its leaves each evening: 'I am, Sir Curly Cabbage, your most humble servant, SAVOY CABBAGE.'"

He had reached this point in his argument when the young boy who had taken our philosopher away brought him back.

"What! Already finished dinner?" my demon cried.

Yes, he replied, all except his dessert: the physiognomist had given him permission to taste ours. Our young host did not wait for me to ask him to explain this mystery.

"I can see," he said, "that this way of life must astonish you. Although in your world you take less care to look after yourselves, the way people take care of themselves in this world is not to be scorned.

"In every house, there is a physiognomist, maintained at public expense: he is more or less what you would call a doctor, except that he looks only after the healthy, and decides how he is going to treat us simply by looking at the proportion, figure and symmetry of our limbs, the lineaments of our face, the colour of our flesh, the delicacy of our skin, the agility of our bodily frame, the sound of our voice, our complexion, and the strength and firmness of our hair. Haven't you ever noticed a rather short man gazing at you for a considerable time? That was the house physiognomist. You can rest assured that, depending on his analysis of your complexion, he will have diversified the exhalations of your dinner. Notice how far the mattress on which you have been set is placed from our beds; he must have judged you to be of a completely different temperament from ours, since he was afraid that the odour evaporating from those little taps on your nose might spread to us, or that ours might waft over to you. You will see him this evening choosing flowers for your bed with the same care and attention."

All the time he was speaking, I was signalling to my host, trying to get him to bring those philosophers round to talking about some aspect of the science they professed. Being a good friend to me, he did so at the earliest opportunity. I will not trouble you with the speeches and prayers that acted as ambassadors to this treaty: the shift from the ridiculous to the sublime was too imperceptible to be depicted. At all events, the last of those doctors, after some talk of this and that, continued in these words:

"It remains for me to prove that there are infinite worlds in one infinite world. So just imagine the universe as one huge animal; the stars, which are worlds, are then other animals inside him, mutually serving as worlds for other peoples (such as ourselves, horses and elephants), while we in turn are also worlds for even smaller people, such as boils, lice, worms and mites. These are an entire earth to other imperceptible creatures, and just as we appear to be a great world for those small folk, perhaps our flesh, blood and vital spirits are nothing other than a whole tissue of tiny animals clustered together, lending us movement from their own, and blindly allowing themselves to be led along by our will acting as their coachman, driving us along ourselves and producing all in concert the action that we call life.

"After all, just tell me this: is it difficult to believe that a louse can imagine a body to be a world, and that when one such louse has travelled from one of your ears to the other, his companions will say of him that he has travelled to the uttermost ends of the world, or that he has covered the distance from one pole to the other? Yes: those tiny folk must take your hair to be the forests of their country, the pores of your skin full of moisture to be springs of water, buboes and mites to be lakes and ponds, abscesses to be seas and fluxions to be floods, and when you comb your hair backwards and forwards, they take this agitation to be the ebbing and flowing of the sea.

"Does not itching prove my point? The mite that causes the itching must surely be one of those tiny animals that has defected from civil society to set up as a tyrant in its own country. If you ask me how it comes about that they are bigger than those other imperceptible little creatures, let me ask you in turn why elephants are bigger than us, and Irishmen bigger than Spaniards? As for that blister and that scab, the reason for which you do not know, they must necessarily come about either when the corpses of the enemies that these tiny giants have slain start to turn putrid, or because the plague produced by the shortage of food (for the rebels have devoured it all) has left heaps of dead bodies to rot over the countryside; or else this tyrant, after driving away his companions who had been blocking the pores of our body with their own bodies, has opened up a passage for the moisture that, by extravasion out of the sphere of our blood's circulation, has become corrupt. Perhaps I will be asked why one mite produces a hundred others? It's not so difficult to imagine; just as one rebellion leads to another, in the same way these little peoples, aroused by the bad example of their seditious companions, each aspire to reign alone, and fan the flames of war, massacre and starvation everywhere. You might object as follows: 'Some people are much less susceptible to itching than others. And yet everyone is equally covered by these tiny animals since it is, so you say, they that create life.' That is true, and it is why we notice that phlegmatic people are less prey to itching than bilious people: these creatures are attuned to the climate in which they live, and thus move more slowly in a cold body than do others that, warmed by the temperature of their region, wriggle and fidget and cannot stay in one place. So the bilious man is much more delicate than the phlegmatic man because there is more animation in the different parts of his body, and since his soul is merely the action of these little creatures, he is able to sense all the places in which the little animals are moving, while the phlegmatic man is not warm enough to arouse much activity outside very few places.

"And if you want further proof of this universal miteyness,* you have only to consider how, when you are wounded, the blood rushes to the wound. Your doctors say that it is guided by nature, which has the foresight to try and come to the aid of the weakened parts, but those are empty imaginings: such a view would imply that, apart from the soul and mind, there is a third intellectual substance in us, with its own functions and organs. It is much easier to believe that, when these tiny animals feel themselves being attacked, they send messengers to their neighbours to ask for help, and that when help starts to arrive from all sides, the country is incapable of supporting so many people, and they are suffocated in the crush, or else die of starvation. This huge death toll occurs when the abscess is ripe; evidence of the fact that these living creatures are then dead lies in the way the flesh goes rotten and can no longer feel. Also, if it frequently happens that the bleeding prescribed to divert the fluxion does some good, this is because those tiny animals have lost many of their comrades in the breach they were trying to close, and so they refuse to assist their allies – they barely have enough power as it is to defend themselves in their own home."

This was his conclusion. And when the second philosopher saw that our eyes were fixed on his, exhorting him to speak in his turn, he said:

"Men, I see that you are eager to teach this little animal, who so resembles us, something of the science that we profess. I am at present dictating a treatise that I would be most happy to show him, because it sheds great light on our physics, being an explanation of the eternal origin of the world. But since I am in a hurry to work on my bellows (for tomorrow, without fail, the city must be up and away), you will have to forgive me for not having the time right now, though I promise that as soon as the city has settled down again, I will satisfy your desires."

At these words, our host's son called his father, and when he arrived, the company asked him the time. The fellow replied, "Eight o'clock." Then his son flew into a rage.

"Ah, you rogue!" he exclaimed. "Didn't I order you to tell us when it was seven o'clock? You know the houses are all leaving tomorrow; the walls have already gone, and your laziness has padlocked your mouth."

"Sir," the fellow replied, "just after you sat down to eat, express orders were given that we must not set out until the day after tomorrow."

"No matter," he retorted, slapping him on the face, "you're supposed to obey blindly, not to question my orders, and you must heed only my commandment. Go and fetch your effigy this very minute."

As soon as he had brought in the effigy, the young man seized it by the arm and gave it a whipping that lasted a good quarter of an hour.

"Now then, you stupid dolt," he continued, "as a punishment for your disobedience, I want you to serve today as a laughing stock for everybody, and so I order you to walk on just two feet for the rest of the day."

The poor old man left the room in tears, and his son continued:

"Gentlemen, please forgive the behaviour of that empty-headed rogue; I had been hoping to make something of him, but he simply took advantage of my friendship. Personally, I think the rascal will be the death of me; to tell you the truth, he has already brought me more than ten times to the point of putting my curse on him."

Although I was biting my lips, I found it extremely difficult not to burst out laughing at this topsy-turvy world. And that is why, so as to interrupt this farcical pedagogy that would prob-ably have ended up by making me split my sides with laughter, I begged him to tell me what he meant by this trip the city was about to take, as he had just said. Were the houses and the walls setting off somewhere? He replied:

"My dear friend, our cities are divided into mobile and sec-ondary; the mobile cities, such as the one in which you are at present, are constructed as follows. The architect constructs each palace, as you can see, from an extremely light wood, and inserts four wheels under them; in the thickness of one of the walls he places several great bellows, the nozzles of which pass horizontally across the top storey, from one gable to the other. In this way, whenever we want to transport the cities to another place (for we give them a change of air every new season), each person unfolds on one side of his lodging several broad sails in front of the bellows; then they wind up a spring to make the bellows play, and in less than a week their houses, blown along by the continuous gusts belched out by those flatulent monsters as they puff out the canvas, can be carried, if so desired, more than a hundred leagues.

"And now for the architecture of the second type of city, called sedentary: the houses are more or less similar to your towers, except that they are made of wood, and pierced through the middle by a big powerful screw that rises from the cellars to the roofs so that they can be raised or lowered at will. The earth underneath is hollowed out to the same depth as the height of the building, and the whole fabric is so constructed that as soon as the frosts start to shiver in the sky, people can lower their houses by turning them round and round to the bottom of the ditch, and, by means of certain great skins with which they cover both the tower and the round hole into which it fits, they can shelter from the inclemency of the air. But as soon as the springtime starts to breathe its gentle breezes and soften the atmosphere, they can come back up into broad daylight thanks to the great screw that I mentioned."

He wanted, I think, to pause for breath just then, and I spoke as follows:

"Upon my word, sir, I would never have been able to believe that such an expert mason could be a philosopher if I did not have you as a witness. That is why, since we are not leaving today, you will have plenty of time to explain the eternal origin of the world to us, as you promised a few moments ago. You have my word that, in return, as soon as I am back home from the moon, as my tutor" (I pointed to my demon) "will bear witness, I will spread your renown, relating all the fine things that you have told me. I can see that you're laughing at this promise, because you do not believe that the moon is a world, and even less that I am one of its inhabitants, but I can assure you that the nations of that world, who consider this one to be merely a moon, will make fun of me when I tell them that their moon is a world, that its fields comprise an earth and that you are people."

His only reply was a smile. Then he spoke in the following terms:

"Since whenever we wish to go back to the origin of this Great All we inevitably encounter three or four absurdities, it is only sensible to take the path that least causes us to stumble: the first obstacle that gives us pause is the eternity of the world, and since men's minds are not strong enough to conceive it, and cannot imagine that this great universe, so beautiful, so well regulated, could have come into being by itself, they resorted to the idea of Creation. But they are like a man who jumps into a river so as to avoid getting drenched in the rain: they are saving themselves from the arms of a dwarf and flinging themselves on the mercy of a giant. And they do not really save themselves, as they grant the eternity of which they deprive the world (since they have not been able to understand it) to God, as if it were easier to imagine it in the latter than in the former. So this absurdity, or this giant that I mentioned, is Creation. After all, tell me truly, has anyone ever been able to conceive how something may come of nothing? Alas! Even between nothing and a single atom there is such an infinite disproportion that the sharpest brain can never grasp it; so, in order to escape from this inexplicable labyrinth, you will have to accept that matter exists eternally with God – and then there will be no need for God, since the world can exist without him. 'But,' you will say, 'even if I grant you that matter is eternal, how did this chaos arrange itself?' Ah, let me explain.

"What you need to imagine, my little animal, is this: first you mentally separate each visible little body into an infinity of invisible little bodies, and then picture to yourself that the infinite universe is composed of nothing other than these infinite atoms, very solid, very incorruptible and very simple – some of them cubic, others shaped like parallelograms, others angular, others round, others pointed, others pyramidal, others hexagonal, others oval: and they all act in different ways, depending on their shape. If you don't believe me, place a perfectly spherical ball of ivory on a very smooth surface: you need give it only the slightest push, and it will roll along for half a quarter of an hour without stopping. Now, if it were as absolutely round as some of the atoms I am talking about, it would never stop. So if art is capable of inclining a body to embark on perpetual motion, why should we not believe that nature cannot do so? The same applies to the other shapes. Some, like the square, require perpetual rest, and some a sideways movement, while others make a half-movement as if jogging on the spot; and when the round shape, whose essence it is to keep moving, is joined to the pyramidal shape, perhaps it adds up to what we call fire, for not only does fire flicker without rest, but it pierces and penetrates all things with ease.

"Over and above that, fire has a different effect depending on how wide and how numerous are the angles to which the round shape is joined: so, for example, the fire of pepper is different from the fire of sugar, the fire of sugar different from that of cinnamon, that of cinnamon different from that of cloves, and this in turn is different from the fire from a bundle of twigs. Now fire, which both builds up and breaks down the universe in its parts and as a whole, has pushed and gathered into an oak all the shapes necessary to make up that oak. 'But,' you will say to me, 'how can chance have assembled in one place all the things that were necessary to produce this oak?' I answer that it is no marvel that matter, arranged in this way, is able to form an oak: it would be much more marvellous if, given the way matter is arranged, the oak had *not* been formed; if certain shapes had been just a little less numerous, it would have been an elm, a poplar, a willow, an elder tree, a sprig of heather or a clump of moss; and if certain shapes had been a little more numerous, it would have been a sensitive plant, an oyster in its shell, a worm, a fly, a frog, a sparrow, a monkey or a man. When you roll three dice on a table and they all turn up twos, or a three, a four and a five, or two sixes and a one, you'll hardly say: 'What a miraculous coincidence! Both dice have come up with the same number, when so many other numbers could have come up! What a miraculous coincidence! Three dice have turned up three successive numbers. What a miraculous coincidence! I have thrown exactly two sixes, and the opposite face of the other six!' I am firmly convinced that, being an intelligent man, you will not utter such exclamations; after all, since there are only a certain quantity of numbers on the dice, it is impossible that one of them will not turn up.

"You are amazed at the way matter, all mixed up any old how, quite at random, can ever form a man, since there were so many things necessary to construct him – but do you not realize that, a hundred million times already, this matter, as it moved towards the shape of a man, has paused to form sometimes a stone, sometimes a lump of lead, sometimes coral, sometimes a flower and sometimes a comet, depending on the excess or lack of certain shapes that were necessary or not necessary to comprise a man? As a result, it is no wonder that, from an infinite quantity of matter changing and shifting without cease, it has contrived to form the few animals, vegetables and minerals that we see, any more than it is any wonder that in a hundred dice throws a royal flush may turn up. It is equally impossible that from this restless movement something will not be made, and this thing will always be admired by some naive fool who does not realize how easy it would have been for it not to be made at all. When the great river of ⊨ turns a mill wheel, or activates the springs of a clock, while the little stream of ⊨ simply runs along and sometimes overflows its banks, you will not tell me that it must be a very intelligent river: after all, you know that it has simply encountered the things that were arranged to create those fine masterpieces; for if it had not come across the mill in its course, the river would not have pulverized the corn; if it had not encountered the clock, it would not have marked the hours; and if the little stream I mentioned had come across the same objects, it would have performed the same miracles. The same applies to fire, which moves by itself; having found the organs required for the agitation necessary for reasoning, it reasoned; when it found the organs required merely for sensing, it sensed; when it found the organs required for vegetating, it vegetated. If you don't believe me, imagine putting out the eyes of the man whom this fire or this soul enables to see, and he will no longer see, just as our great river will no longer mark the hours if the clock is destroyed.

"Finally, these first indivisible atoms form a circle over which the most perplexing difficulties of physics can smoothly roll.

Even the operation of the senses, that nobody hitherto has managed to understand, is something I can explain perfectly easily by means of these little bodies. Let's begin with sight: as it is the most incomprehensible, it merits our attention first.

"So, in my view, sight occurs when the membranes covering the eye, whose openings are similar to those of glass, transmit outwards the fire-dust that we call visual rays; this dust is stopped by an opaque matter that forces it to rebound to its origin. For, encountering on its route the image of the object that has thrown it back – an image that is merely an infinite number of small bodies continuously being exhaled in equal surface areas from the object being looked at – the fire-dust carries the image to our eye.

"Of course you will object that glass is a dense, opaque body, and yet instead of throwing back those other little bodies, it allows itself to be pierced by them. My answer is that the pores of glass are shaped like the atoms of the fire crossing it, and that just as a wheat sieve is no use for sieving oats, nor an oat sieve for sieving wheat, in the same way a pinewood box, however thin, which allows sound to escape, is not penetrable to sight, and a piece of crystal, however transparent, which can be pierced by sight, is not penetrable to hearing."

At this point I simply had to interrupt him.

"But how, sir," I asked him, "can you explain on the basis of those principles how it is that we are depicted in a mirror?"

"It is perfectly easy," he replied. "Just imagine that the fires from our eyes have crossed the glass and encounter behind it an adiaphanous body that bounces them back, so they return the same way they came; when they find the tiny bodies that have left our body travelling in equal surface areas spread across the mirror, they bring them back to our eyes; and our imagination, which is warmer than the other faculties of the soul, attracts the most subtle of them, and from them creates a small-scale portrait.

"The operation of hearing is no more difficult to understand. I will keep it succinct: let us consider hearing simply from the point of view of harmony. So imagine a lute plucked by the hands of a master of the art. You will ask me how I can possibly become aware of something so far away from me that I do not even see it. Do sponges emerge from my ears to drink in this music and transmit it back to me? Or does the player engender in my head another little player with a little lute, and then command him to sing me the same tune? No; this miracle proceeds rather from the fact that, when the string is plucked and strikes the tiny bodies of which the air is composed, it projects it into my brain, gently piercing it with these tiny corporeal bodies, and depending on the tension in the string, the sound is high, because it pushes the atoms more vigorously; and the organ being penetrated in this way provides our imagination with sufficient material to create a picture; if there is not enough tension, the result is that our memory has still not completed its image; we are thus obliged to repeat the same sound to it, so that, from the materials providing it for example with the bars of a sarabande, it will take enough to complete the portrait of that same sarabande.

"But this operation is next to nothing; the wonder is that, thanks to its ministry, we are moved sometimes to joy, sometimes to rage, sometimes to pity, sometimes to reverie and sometimes to sorrow. I imagine this happens when the movement to which these tiny bodies are subjected encounters inside us other tiny bodies all being moved in the same way, or else their own shape makes them susceptible to the same agitation; for in that case, the newcomers rouse their hosts to move as they are moving. In this way, when some violent air encounters the fire of our blood inclined to the same agitation, it excites this fire to erupt outwards, and this is what we call 'the ardour of courage'. If the sound is milder and does not have the strength to arouse anything more than a gentler and less agitated flame (for matter is more volatile as it leads the flame along the nerves, membranes and the pores of our flesh), it arouses the tickling that we call 'joy'. The same applies to the bubbling and boiling of the other passions, depending on whether these tiny bodies are flung more or less violently against us, depending also on the movement they receive when they encounter other agitations, and depending finally on what they stir within us. That is how hearing works.

"Now for the sense of touch, which is no more difficult to demonstrate. From all palpable matter there arises a perpetual emission of tiny bodies; whenever we touch this matter, they evaporate in greater quantity because we squeeze them out of the object being handled, like water from a sponge. Hard bodies report their solidity to the organ of touch; supple bodies report their softness; uneven bodies their roughness; burning bodies their heat; and freezing bodies their ice. In proof of this, we are not so sensitive at discerning things by touching them with hands that are worn out by hard work, because of the thick calluses which, being neither porous, nor animate, find it difficult to transmit those vaporous fumes of matter. The question will no doubt be raised: where does the organ of touch have its seat? In my opinion, it is spread throughout the whole surface of the mass, seeing as it occurs through the mediation of the nerves of which our skin is merely an imperceptible and continuous tissue. Nonetheless, I imagine that the closer the limb with which we are feeling is to our head, the more quickly we can distinguish things; this can be shown by experience when, eyes closed, we run a hand over something, since we immediately guess its identity – whereas, if we touch it with our feet, it takes a long time to work out what it is. This is a result of the fact that, since our skin is covered all over with tiny holes, our nerves, the matter of which is not any denser, leave behind a great number of those tiny atoms in the small channels of their texture before they reach the brain, where their journey ends.

"It simply remains for me to prove that smell and taste also come about thanks to the operation of the same tiny bodies.

"So tell me then, when I taste food, is it not because of the moistness of the mouth melting it? You have to admit that, since there are various salts in a pear, which, by being

dissolved, separate out into tiny bodies of a shape different from those which compose the savour of a plum, they
necessarily pierce our palate in a completely different way;
just as the deep scar left by the iron point of a pike thrust
into me is quite different from the pain inflicted by the
sudden impact of a bullet from a pistol, and as the bullet
of a pistol imprints on me a pain different from that of a
steel square.*

"Of smell I have nothing to say, since even your philosophers
admit that this comes about through the continual emission of
tiny bodies detaching themselves from their mass and coming
to strike our noses as they pass by.

"On the basis of this principle I am going to explain to you
the creation, harmony and influence of the celestial globes with
the immutable variety of the meteors."

He was about to continue, but our old host entered, and the
philosopher decided it was time to withdraw. He brought with
him crystals full of glow-worms to lighten up the room, but as
these little insect fires lose a great deal of their radiance when
they are not freshly picked, these ones, being ten days old, gave
off almost no flame.

My demon did not allow the company to be inconvenienced
by this for long; he went up to his little room, and came down
immediately with two balls of fire so brilliant that everyone
expressed astonishment that he was not burning his fingers.

"These incombustible torches," he said, "will be of more
help to us than your globes of glow-worms. They are rays of
sunlight that I have purged of their heat, for otherwise the cor-
rosive qualities of the sun's fire would have dazzled you and
damaged your sight. I captured its light and enclosed it within
the transparent balls that I am holding. This should be no great
cause of wonder to you, as it is no more difficult for me, who
was born in the sun, to condense the rays of light that are the
dust of that world than it is for you to pick up dust or atoms
that are the pulverized earth of this world."

When the praises of this child of the sun had been sufficiently sung, the young host sent his father to see the two philosophers home, with a dozen globes of glow-worms hanging from his four feet. As for the rest of us, namely the young host, my tutor and myself, we went to bed on the orders of the physiognomist.

This time he put me in a room of violets and lilies, and had me tickled in the usual way to lull me to sleep, and the next day, at nine o'clock, I saw my demon come in. He told me he had come from the Palace, where ▆▆, one of the Queen's ladies, had sent for him; she had enquired after me, and insisted that she still intended to keep her word to me – namely that she would be all too happy to follow me if I would take her with me to the other world.

"What I found particularly edifying," he continued, "was when I realized that the main purpose of the journey was none other than that of becoming a Christian. So I promised to help her achieve her aim with all my strength, and to invent for this purpose a machine capable of holding three or four people, in which you will be able to rise together. This very day I am going to embark seriously on the execution of this enterprise: that is why, so as to amuse yourself while I am no longer with you, I have here a book that I will leave you. I brought it with me once upon a time from my native land; it is entitled *The States and Empires of the Sun*.* And I am also giving you this one, which I rate much more highly; it is the *Great Work of the Philosophers*,* which one of the most intelligent spirits of the sun has composed. In it, he proves that everything is true, and sets out the way of physically uniting the truths in every contradiction, showing for instance that white is black and black is white; that it is possible to be and not to be at the same time; that nothingness is something, and that all things that are are not. But note that he proves these novel paradoxes quite without any tortuous logic or sophistry. Whenever you get bored reading it, you can go for a walk or have a chat with our young host, your companion: his mind has many charms; what I dislike about him is the fact that he is irreligious, but if he happens to shock you, or to bring up arguments that make your faith totter, do not fail to come and set them out before me straight away, and I will resolve every difficulty. Anyone else would order you to break off all dealings with anyone attempting to philosophize on such subjects, but he is extremely vain, and I am sure that he would take such flight as a defeat, and would imagine that your belief is contrary to reason if you refused to listen to his arguments. Remember to live freely."

Having said this, he left me, for this turn of phrase is the farewell with which, in that country, you take leave of someone, just as our "good day" or "your servant, sir" are there expressed by this compliment: "Love me, you wise man, as I love you". Hardly had he gone than I started to peruse my books. The boxes they were in – in other words, their covers – seemed to me admirable in their richness; the one was carved from a single diamond, incomparably more brilliant than those in our world; the second seemed merely to be a monstrous pearl split into two. My demon had translated these books into the language of this world, but as I have not yet spoken about their printing, I'll explain how these two volumes had been put together.

At the opening of the box I found inside a certain metal construction quite similar to our clocks, filled with countless little springs and imperceptible machines. It is indeed a book – but a miraculous book with neither pages nor letters; in short, it is a book for which, if you want to learn from it, your eyes are of no use; you simply need your ears. So when someone wishes to read, he winds this machine up with a great number of keys of every kind; then he turns the needle to the chapter he wishes to listen to, and thereupon there emerges from this nutshell, as from a man's mouth or a musical instrument, all the different and distinct sounds that are used as a form of linguistic expression between the moon's aristocratic inhabitants.

When I had pondered at length this most marvellous way of making books, I was no longer surprised to see that the young men in this country knew more things at the age of sixteen or eighteen than do the greybeards in ours; after all, since they can read as soon as they can speak, they are never short of reading matter; sitting in their rooms, taking a stroll, travelling both on foot and on horseback, they can have in their pockets, or hanging from the pommels of their saddles, thirty of these books, and they merely have to wind up the springs on them to hear just one chapter, or else several, if they are in the mood to listen to a whole book: in this way you are never without the company of all the great men, both living and dead, conversing with you viva voce.

This present kept me occupied for more than an hour, and finally, having attached the books to my ears like earrings, I went out for a stroll through the city. And I had not gone down the road opposite our house when at the far end I encountered a rather large gathering of sad-looking people.

Four of them were bearing on their shoulders a kind of coffin draped in black. I asked a spectator what was the meaning of this procession, similar to the funerals in my country; he told me that the wicked ━▪━, whose name was signified by people giving a flick of their fingers to their right knees, had been convicted of envy and ingratitude and had passed away yesterday; Parliament had sentenced him over twenty years ago to die a natural death in his bed and then to be buried after his death. I started to laugh at this reply, and when he asked me why, I replied as follows:

"You surprise me when you say that what is the mark of blessing in our world – namely a long life, a peaceful death and a dignified burial – serves in this world as an exemplary punishment."

"What! You take burial to be a mark of blessing!" the man retorted. "Ah, good Heavens, can you think of anything more dreadful than a corpse heaving with the worms that swarm all over it, at the mercy of the toads that gnaw at its cheeks – in short, the plague itself, dressed in the body of a man? Good God!

The mere thought of having, even when dead, my face wrapped in a cloth and a clod of earth stopping my mouth almost makes me suffocate! The wretch you see being carried along there was sentenced, over and above the infamy of being thrown into a ditch, to have a hundred and fifty of his friends present at his funeral procession, and these in turn were commanded, as a punishment for having taken a liking to an envious and ungrateful man, to appear at his funeral with sad faces – and had it not been for judges taking pity on him, imputing his crimes in part to his lack of intelligence, they would have ordered those friends to weep at the ceremony. Apart from criminals, everybody is cremated: and this is a very honourable and reasonable custom, since we believe that fire, having separated the pure from the impure, and from its heat gathered by sympathy that natural heat that constituted the soul, gives it the strength to continue rising upwards to some star, the abode of certain peoples more immaterial than ourselves, and more intellectual, because their temperament must correspond to and participate in the purity of the globe that they inhabit, and this radical flame, having been rectified even more by the subtlety of the elements of that world, finally composes one of the citizens of that flaming land.

"And yet even this is not our best way of burying people. When one of our philosophers has reached an age where he feels his mind growing weak and the ice of the years numbing the movements of his soul, he gathers his friends together for a sumptuous banquet. Then, having set out the reasons that have led him to resolve to take leave of nature, and his lack of any great hope of being able to add much to the fine actions he has performed, he is either shown mercy (in other words, ordered to die), or severity (and commanded to live). And when, by majority vote, his life has been placed within his own hands, he informs his nearest and dearest of the day and the place: his friends purge themselves and abstain from eating for twenty-four hours; then, when they arrive at the dwelling of this wise man, they sacrifice to the sun and enter the room where the noble fellow awaits them, reposing upon a ceremonial bed. Everyone rushes forwards, in accordance with their rank, to embrace him, and when it is the turn of the man he loves the most, he first kisses him tenderly, then draws him down onto his stomach and, joining his mouth to his friend's mouth, with his free right hand, he plunges a dagger into his own heart's blood. The other does not detach his lips from the lips of his lover until he senses him expiring; then he pulls out the weapon from his breast and, with his mouth closing the wound, swallows his blood and continues sucking until he can drink no more. Thereupon, another succeeds him while the former is taken to bed. When the second is sated, he is taken to bed to give place to a third. Finally, once the whole assembly has drunk its fill, after four or five hours they bring to each man a girl of sixteen or seventeen years, and for the next three or four days they enjoy the pleasures of love, their only nourishment being the flesh of the dead man, which they are given to eat completely raw, so that, if from their embraces something may be born, they may be assured that it is their friend coming back to life."

I did not waste any more time listening to this man, but left him there and continued my stroll.

Although I did not go for a very long walk, the time I employed observing the details of the spectacles and visiting various places in town was the reason why I arrived more than two hours after dinner had been prepared. They asked me why I was so late.

"It's not my fault," I replied to the cook, who was complaining. "Several times, I asked people in the streets what time it was, but their only reply was to open their mouths, clench their teeth and twist their faces into a weird grimace!"

"What!" the whole company exclaimed. "Don't you realize that this was their way of telling you the time?"

"Good Heavens," I replied, "they could have stuck their big noses out into the sunshine and I still wouldn't have known what time it was."

"It's very convenient," they told me. "It enables them to get by without a clock, since they use their teeth as such a perfect sundial that when they want to tell someone what time it is, they simply open their lips, and the shadow of their noses falling across their teeth marks the time as if on a sundial, so they can reply to anyone asking them for the time. And now for the reason why everyone in this country has a big nose: as soon as a woman has given birth, the midwife takes the child to the prior of the seminary; after exactly one year, the experts gather, and if his nose is found to be shorter than a certain length maintained by the syndic, he is deemed to be snub-nosed and handed over to the priests, who castrate him. Perhaps you will ask the reason for this barbarous behaviour – how can it be that we, for whom virginity is a crime, forcibly make certain people chaste? The reason we do this is that we have observed over the last thirty centuries that a big nose is a sign over our door that says: 'Herein resides a man who is witty, prudent, courteous, affable, noble-hearted and liberal' – and that a small nose is the cork of the opposite vices. That is why we make eunuchs of the snub-nosed, because the Republic prefers not to have any children from them, rather than to have children who will resemble them."

He was still speaking when I saw a man come in completely naked. I immediately sat down and put on my hat to do him honour, for these are the marks of the greatest respect that you can show anyone in this country.

"It is the Kingdom's wish," he said, "that you should warn the magistrates before departing for your country, because a mathematician has just promised the Council that if, once you are back in your world, you are prepared to construct a certain machine that he will teach you how to make – corresponding with one he will keep ready in this world – he will draw your world to him and join it to our globe."

As soon as he had left, I addressed the young host in these terms:

"Ah, I beg you, please tell me the meaning of that piece of bronze shaped like a man's genitals dangling from his belt."

I had already seen several of these things at court when I lived in a cage, but because I was almost always surrounded by the Queen's ladies, I was afraid of violating the respect owed to their sex and their condition if in their presence I brought the conversation round to such a vulgar subject.

"Females here are not, any more than are the males, so ungrateful as to blush at the sight of that which has forged them, and virgins are not ashamed to love, in memory of their mother nature, the only part of our bodies that bears nature's name.

"Know then that the sash with which this man is honoured, and from which there hangs a medal in the shape of a virile member, is the symbol of a gentleman, and the mark that distinguishes the nobleman from the commoner."

I have to confess that this paradox struck me as so bizarre that I could not keep from laughing.

"This custom strikes me as completely extraordinary," I told my little host, "for in our world, it is wearing a sword that is the mark of nobility."

He showed no surprise at this, but exclaimed:

"Oh my little man, the noblemen in your world must be crazy if they parade around an instrument that designates an executioner, and is forged only in order to destroy us – is indeed the sworn enemy of everything that lives – while on the other hand, they conceal that without which we would be reduced to the rank of non-being, the Prometheus of every animal, and the indefatigable repairer of nature's weaknesses! Unhappy land, where the marks of generation are viewed as ignominious, and those of annihilation are held in honour! And yet you call that member 'the part of shame',* as if there were anything more glorious than giving life, and anything more infamous than taking it away!"

Throughout this conversation, we did not stop eating, and as soon as we had arisen from our beds, we went out into the garden to take the air.

The order and beauty of the place beguiled us for a while, but since the noblest desire that tickled me at the time was to convert to religion a soul so greatly elevated above the vulgar, I exhorted him again and again not to besmirch with matter the noble genius with which Heaven had provided him, and to save from the crush of animals a spirit capable of the vision of God; in a word, I adjured him to ensure that one day his immortality would be united to pleasure rather than to pain.

"What!" he replied, bursting out laughing. "You deem your souls to be immortal while those of the beasts are not? To tell you the truth, my good friend, your pride is most insolent! Please explain your arguments for thinking that you are immortal and the beasts are not. Might it be because we are endowed with reasoning and they are not? To begin with, I deny as much, and I will prove to you whenever you like that they can reason just as we can. But even if it were true that reason had been given us as an inheritance apart, and that it was a privilege reserved to our species alone, does this mean that God is obliged to enrich man with immortality because he has already lavished reason upon him? In that case would I not be obliged to give a pistole to that poor man today because I gave him an *écu* yesterday?* You yourself can easily see the illogicality here. On the contrary – if I am going to be fair, then, rather than giving this man a pistole, I should give the other man an *écu*, since he has received nothing from me. The inevitable conclusion, my dear companion, is that God, who is a thousand times fairer than we are, cannot have poured out all his benefits on some creatures, only to leave nothing to the others. Perhaps you will quote the example of the elder sons in your world, who sweep up almost all the goods of the household as their share, but this is a failing of your fathers, who, wishing to perpetuate their names, were afraid these names might be lost or fade away in poverty. But God, who is quite incapable of error, was careful not to commit an error of such magnitude – and then, since in God's eternity there is neither before nor after, younger brothers are to his eyes no younger than elder brothers."

I will not hide the fact that this line of reasoning rather shook me.

"With your permission," I told him, "I will break off at this point, since I do not feel strong enough to reply to you; I'll go and find out the solution to this difficulty from our common tutor."

Without waiting for him to reply, I immediately went up to the room of that clever demon, and, without further ado, I told him how someone had just objected to my belief in the immortality of our souls. This is what he replied:

"My son, that young hothead was very keen to persuade you that it is implausible that man's soul is immortal because this would make God unjust – and He who is called the common father of all beings would then have given an advantage to one species and abandoned each and every other one to nothingness or misfortune. And these reasons do indeed seem alluring when seen from afar. And although I could well ask him how exactly he knows that what is just in our eyes is also just in God's, how he knows that God is measured by our standards, how he knows that our laws and our customs, which were established only to remedy our disorders, also serve to chop into little pieces God's omnipotence, I will pass over all these things and all the divine replies that the fathers of your Church have made on the subject, and I will uncover to you a mystery that has not yet been revealed:

"You know, my son, that by the earth a tree is nourished, by the tree a pig, and by the pig a man. So can we not believe, since all the beings in nature tend to the most perfect, that they aspire to become men, whose essence is the consummation of the finest and best imagined mixture in the world, being the only one that links the life of the brutes with that of the angels? That these metamorphoses happen, only a narrow-minded fellow would deny. Do you not see that an apple tree, by the heat of its germ, as if through a mouth, sucks and digests the grass that surrounds it; that a pig devours this fruit and turns it into a part of itself;

and that a man, eating the pig, heats up this dead flesh, joins it to itself and finally enables this animal to live again in the form of a nobler species? Thus that great pontiff that you see crowned with a mitre was only sixty years ago a clump of grass in my garden. So, as God is the common father of all these creatures, assuming he loves them all equally, it can easily be imagined how, thanks to this metempsychosis that is more reasonable than the Pythagorean version, everything that feels and everything which vegetates, indeed all matter, will pass through man – and then that great day of judgement will arrive, being the aim to which tend the secrets of the prophets and all their philosophy."

I came down into the garden fully satisfied, and was just beginning to recite to my companion what our master had taught me when the physiognomist arrived to take us to dinner and then to the dormitory. I will not dwell on the details, and merely say that I was fed and put to bed as on the previous day.

The next day, as soon as I was awake, I went to rouse my antagonist.

"It is as great a miracle," I told him as I went over to him, "to find a mind as powerful as yours buried in sleep as it is to see a fire lying inactive."

He smiled at this clumsy compliment.

"But," he exclaimed in a passion of anger and love, "will you never rid your mouth as well as your reason of that fantastical term 'miracle'? Know that those names defame the name of a philosopher. Since the wise man sees nothing in the world that he cannot conceive or that he cannot judge of being conceived, he should abominate all those expressions – 'miracles', 'prodigies', 'events against nature' – they have been invented by the stupid to excuse the weakness of their understanding."

Whereupon I felt obliged in all conscience to disabuse him, and answered in these words:

"Even if you do not believe in miracles, they occur nonetheless – very frequently. I have seen some with my own eyes. I have known more than twenty sick people to be miraculously cured."

"You say," he interrupted, "that those people were cured by miracle, but you do not know that the force of imagination is capable of combating every illness thanks to a certain natural balm spread throughout our bodies containing every quality contrary to those of all the ills that assail us: and our imagination, alerted by pain, chooses the specific remedy that it then opposes to the poison and cures us. Hence it is that the most skilful doctor in our world advises the patient to take for preference an ignorant doctor whom he judges to be highly skilled rather than a highly skilled doctor whom he judges to be ignorant, because in his view our imagination works on our health; so long as it is aided by remedies, it is capable of curing us – but the most powerful remedies are not strong enough if imagination does not apply them! Are you surprised that the first men in our world lived for so many centuries without having any knowledge of medicine? Their nature was strong, and that universal balm was not dissipated by the drugs that your doctors force you to consume. In order to begin their cure, they needed merely to wish with all the power of their imagination that they already had been cured. Immediately their fantasy – clear, vigorous and thrusting – plunged into that vital oil, applied the active to the passive, and almost in the twinkling of an eye, they were just as healthy as before. Of course, such amazing cures still happen today, but ordinary folk put them down as miracles.

"Personally I do not believe in them at all, and my reason is that it is easier to think that all of those chatterers are wrong than that a miracle actually happens. I will put this question to them, for example: take that man suffering from fever who has just recovered – throughout his illness, he doubtless wished to be well again; he made vows to this end. Now it is necessary that, being ill, he must either die, or else remain ill, or else get better. If he had died, people would have said that God had chosen to recompense him for his pains; perhaps they will make God equivocate maliciously, saying that he heard the patient's prayers and cured him of all his ills. If he had remained in his infirmity, they would have said that he did not have faith; but, just because he has been cured, it is an obvious miracle. Is it not much more likely that his fantasy, excited by a violent desire for health, carried out this operation? I agree that many of those gentlemen who have made vows have indeed recovered, but how many more do we see who, for all their vows, have perished wretchedly?"

"But at least," I replied, "if what you say of this balm is true, it is a mark of the rational nature of our soul, since, without using the instruments of our reason, nor relying on any help from our will, our soul knows independently, as if it were quite outside us, how to apply active to passive. Now if, being separate from us, it is rational, it must necessarily be spiritual; and if you admit that it is spiritual, I conclude that it is immortal, since death happens to animals only through a change in the shapes of which matter alone is capable."

The young man then sat up in bed and, making me sit down on it, spoke to me more or less in the following terms:

"As regards the soul of animals, which is corporeal, I'm not surprised that it should die, seeing that it may well be nothing but a harmony of the four qualities, a force of the blood, a proportion between organs acting in concert; but I am greatly astonished that our soul, incorporeal, intellectual and immortal, should be obliged to leave our bodies for the same reasons that make the soul of an ox perish. Has it made a pact with our body that, if there is a sword thrust to our heart, a lead bullet in our brain or a musket shot through our body, it is to abandon its ruined house straight away? If so, it would often be breaking its contract, for some men die of a wound from which others recover; every soul would need to have come to a different arrangement with its body. The truth is that the soul, which has so much intelligence – or at least so we are told – is enraged at having to leave its dwelling when it sees that it is going to be shown straight to its new apartment in hell. And if this soul were spiritual, and of itself reasonable, as they say, so that it were just

95

as capable of intelligence when separated from our corporeal mass as when still lodged within it, why is it that those who are born blind, with all the splendid advantages of that intellectual soul, cannot even imagine what it is to see? Why cannot the deaf hear? Is it because death has not yet deprived them of all their senses? What! Does this mean I cannot use my right hand because I also have a left hand? In order to prove that the soul cannot act without the senses, despite being spiritual, they put forward the example of a painter who cannot paint a picture if he does not have any brushes. Yes, but this does not mean that the painter who cannot work without any brushes will be able to produce better work when, along with his brushes, he has also lost his paints, his pencils, his canvases and his paint pots as well. On the contrary! The more obstacles there are hindering his labour, the more impossible it will be for him to paint. And yet they claim that the soul, which can act only imperfectly when it loses just one of its tools in the course of life, will work perfectly when, after our death, it has lost all of its tools. If they insist that the soul does not need these instruments to perform its functions, I will insist that they ought to whip those in the Quinze-Vingts hospice* who pretend they can see nothing."

"But," I told him, "if our soul died – and that is the conclusion I can see you wish to draw – the resurrection that we expect would be nothing but an empty fancy, for God would have to recreate the soul, and that would not be a resurrection."

He interrupted me, shaking his head.

"Heavens above!" he exclaimed. "Who has lulled you with such a fairy tale? What! *You?* What! *Me?* What! *My servant girl* – resurrected?"

"It is no mere fable," I replied. "It is an indubitable truth that I will now prove to you."

"And I," he said, "will prove the contrary.

"To begin with, then, let us suppose that you eat a Mohammedan; in this way, you convert him into your substance! Is it not true that this Mohammedan, being digested, will turn partly into flesh, partly into blood and partly into sperm? You will embrace your wife, and from the semen, drawn entirely from the Mohammedan's corpse, you cast the mould of a fine young Christian. My question is this: will the Mohammedan have his body? If the earth gives it back to him, the little Christian will not have *his* body, since he is nothing but a part of the Mohammedan. If you tell me that the little Christian will have *his* body, that means that God will steal from the Mohammedan what the Christian has received only from the Mohammedan. And so it is absolutely inevitable that one or the other will lack a body! Perhaps you will reply that God will reproduce matter to make up a body for the one who does not have enough? Yes, but then another difficulty arises – namely that when the damned Mohammedan arises, and God provides him with a brand-new body because his has been stolen away by the Christian, the body alone, like a soul alone, does not comprise a man: you need both these parts to be joined together in a single subject, and as body and soul are equally integral parts of man, if God fashions for this Mohammedan another body than his, he is no longer the same individual. Thus God is damning another man than the one who has merited hell; thus it is this body that has played the lecher, this body that has criminally abused all of its senses, and yet God, to chastise this body, hurls *another* body into the fire – a body that is virgin and pure, and has never lent its organs to the operation of the slightest crime. And what really would be ridiculous is that this body would have merited hell and paradise at one and the same time, for, in so far as it is a Mohammedan, it must be damned; in so far as it is a Christian, it must be saved. As a result, God can place it in paradise only by being unjust, rewarding the damnation it had merited as a Mohammedan with glory, and can hurl it into hell only by being equally unjust, rewarding with eternal death the beatitude that it had merited as a Christian. Thus, if he wishes to be equitable, God must both eternally damn that man and save him."

I replied in these terms:

"Ah, there is nothing I can say in reply to your sophistical arguments against the resurrection, except that God has declared it, and God cannot lie."

"Don't go so fast," he replied. "You have already got to 'God has said it'; you first need to prove that there is a God, for I personally deny it straight."

"I will not waste time reciting to you the evident demonstrations that the philosophers have used to establish this," said I. "I would need to repeat everything that reasonable men have ever written. I will simply ask you what risk you run by believing it; I am fully assured that you cannot think of a single one. So, since this belief cannot fail to be useful, why are you not convinced of it? For if there is a God, apart from the fact that if you do not believe in him you will have made a mistake, you will also have disobeyed the precept that commands you to believe in him; and if there is no God, you will be no better off than us!"*

"Oh," he replied, "but I *will* be better off than you, for if there is no God, the argument between you and me results in a tie; but on the contrary, if there is a God, I cannot possibly have offended something that I believed did not exist, since, in order to sin, one must do so either knowingly or willingly. Surely you can see that a man, even one of no great intelligence, would not be angry if a porter insulted him if the porter had not meant to do so, mistaking him for someone else, or speaking in those terms because he was drunk? A fortiori, will God, who is immutable, fly into a rage with us for not knowing him, since it was he himself who refused to give us the means of knowing him? Good Heavens, my little animal, if believing in God were so necessary to us, if it were a matter of our eternity, no less, would not God himself have infused within us all a light as clear as the sun, hidden from nobody? To pretend that he has chosen to play hide and seek with men,* saying as children do – 'Found you!' – means that he sometimes masks himself and sometimes unmasks himself, disguises himself from some men to manifest himself to others; it is to forge for oneself a God who is either stupid or malicious, seeing that if it is by the force of my genius that I have known him, it is he who merits and not myself, since he could have given me a soul or organs too feeble to enable me to recognize him. And if, on the contrary, he had given me a mind incapable of understanding him, it would not have been my fault but his, since he could have given me a mind quick enough to understand him."

These diabolical, ridiculous opinions made me shudder from head to toe. As I started to examine this man with rather more attention, I was dumbfounded to notice in his face something frightful that I had not yet perceived: his eyes were small and deep-set, his complexion dark, his mouth big, his chin hairy and his fingernails black. "Oh God," I immediately thought, "this wretch is already damned while still alive, and he may even be the Antichrist who is so much spoken of in our world."

But I did not want to reveal my thoughts to him, because of the esteem in which I held his intelligence, and indeed the favourable aspects with which nature had gazed on his cradle and led me to conceive some friendship for him. But I was unable to contain myself entirely and suddenly broke out in imprecations, threatening him with a bad end. But he cast my anger back at me: "Yes!" he exclaimed, "by the death…" I do not know what he intended to say, because just at this moment there was a knock at the door of my room, and in came a tall, black, hairy man. He came across to us, and, seizing the blasphemer by the waist, he carried him off towards the chimney.

The pity I felt at the fate of that wretch gave me no choice but to hold tight to him and try to drag him from the claws of the Ethiopian, but the latter was so powerful that he carried us both off, and on an instant we were up in the clouds. It was no longer love for my neighbour that obliged me to cling to him so tightly, but fear of falling. After having flown through the sky for I do not know how many days, without any idea of what would become of me, I realized that I was approaching our world. Already I could distinguish Asia from Europe and Europe from Africa. Already my eyes, as I flew lower, could not see beyond Italy, and my heart told me that this devil was doubtless carrying my host down to hell, body and soul, and it was for this reason that he was passing through our earth, because hell is at its centre. However, I forgot these thoughts and everything that had happened to me since the devil had been our vehicle, as I was suddenly overcome by terror at the sight of a mountain all in flames that I almost touched. This blazing spectacle made me cry out, "Jesu Maria!" I had barely uttered the last letter than I found myself spreadeagled on the heather at the top of a small hill and two or three shepherds around me reciting the litany and speaking Italian to me. "Oh!" I exclaimed then, "God be praised! So I have finally found Christians in the world of the moon. Tell me, my friends, in which province of your world am I now?"

"In Italy," they replied.

"What!" I interrupted. "Is there also an Italy in the world of the moon?"

I had still not had time to reflect on this latest incident, and so still had not noticed that they were speaking Italian to me, and that I was replying to them in the same language.

So when I was completely disabused and nothing prevented me from acknowledging that I was back in this world, I allowed myself to be led to where these peasants wished to take me. But I had not yet arrived at the gates of —— when all the dogs in the town rushed up towards me, and if my fear had not dragged me into a house where I barred the door against them, I would most certainly have been eaten alive.

A quarter of an hour later, as I rested in this house, lo and behold there was, on every side, a witches' sabbath of every dog, I believe, in the kingdom; every kind from a bulldog to lapdog could be seen, howling in the most dreadful fury as if they were celebrating the birthday of their first Adam.

This turn of events caused no little surprise to all the people who saw it, but when I started to turn my thoughts in more detail to this adventure, I soon decided that these animals were enraged with me because of the world from which I came. "For," I said to myself, "as they are accustomed to bay at the moon because of the pain she inflicts on them from such a distance, doubtless they wanted to fling themselves on me because I smell of the moon whose odour annoys them."

To purge myself of this unwholesome air, I exposed myself completely naked in the sunshine lying on a terrace. I spent four or five hours sunbathing there, at the end of which I came down, and the dogs, no longer smelling the influence that had turned me into their enemy, all returned to their separate homes.

I went to the harbour to enquire when a vessel would be leaving for France, and, once I was embarked, my mind was entirely occupied with ruminating over the marvels of my journey. A thousand times over I was filled with wonder at the providence of God, who had sequestered these men, so naturally irreligious, in a place where they could not corrupt his beloved creatures, and punished them for their pride by abandoning them to their own conceit. Thus I have no doubt that he has waited until now to send someone to preach the Gospel to them because he knew that they would abuse it, and that their resistance would merely serve to earn them a harsher punishment in the other world.

Note on the text

I have used the French text *Voyage dans la Lune*, ed. by Maurice Laugaa (Paris: Garnier-Flammarion, 1970), but have also consulted the critical edition by Madeleine Alcover (Paris: Champion, 1970). I have used the musical notation from the first edition (Paris: Charles de Sercy, 1657).

Notes

p. 2, *the works of Cardano*: Girolamo Cardano (1501–76) was an Italian mathematician, astrologer and algebraist. Forever short of funds, he made money by gambling and playing chess. He was accused of heresy for casting Jesus's horoscope. His heterodoxy will have appealed to Cyrano.

p. 2, *he writes that... the moon*: Possibly a reminiscence of Cardano's encyclopedic work *De subtilitate*, or *On Subtlety* (1550), which relates that Cardano's father saw seven men with "subtle bodies" appear to him one summer's evening in 1491 (though he does not claim that they came from the moon), and talked with them for over three hours.

p. 3, *God had... noble enterprise*: Possibly an echo of the occasion on which God made the sun (and the moon) stand still so that Joshua could win the Battle of Ajalon also known as Aijalon: see Joshua 10:11–14, especially verse 12: "Sun, stand thou still upon Gibeon; and thou, Moon, in the valley of Aijalon." This verse was often quoted as evidence against the Copernican theory, for if the sun were instructed to stand still, it could not already *be* still; i.e. it did after all move round the earth, as in the old Ptolemaic system.

p. 4, *M. de Montbazon*: The Governor of Paris until 1650.

p. 4, *New France*: Nouvelle France was the name of the French domains in present-day Canada, and Charles Huault de Montmagny was the Viceroy of Quebec from 1636 to 1647.

p. 6, *your eccentrics... epicycles*: These are all terms used in the Ptolemaic attempt to transcribe the orbits of the planets in such a way that they could be seen as orbiting round the earth. The system of Copernicus, although heliocentric, in fact preserved many of the Ptolemaic cycles.

p. 7, *books by Gassendi*: Pierre Gassendi (1592–1655) attacked Aristotle: he was a follower of Epicurus, and tried to reconcile the latter's ideas with Christianity. He made many useful observations of the sun (including sunspots – which caused dismay, as the sun was supposed to be perfect) and the planets.

p. 8, *I believe... reach us*: This view of the universe as an immense conglomeration of solar systems stretching away into vast distances was in Cyrano's time new and, for many, alarming.

p. 8, *housebreaker... down the street*: The word *"crocheteur"* can mean a porter, but also – as I have translated it here – a housebreaker or picklock.

p. 13, *influence*: In the old astrological sense – a supposed fluid flowing from the stars and affecting the lives of those below.

p. 15, *The animals... the Antipodes*: The animals – more rational than those on earth, perhaps, in so far as they are capable of being disconcerted by the paradoxes of appearance – see the sun's reflection "down there" in the "Antipodes" of the river water while the sun itself is still high in the sky.

p. 17, *The odour... me*: This verse does not exist as such in the Bible: Cyrano may have forged a sentence of his own. Similar thoughts are expressed in, for example, Psalm 141:2, "Let my prayer be set forth before thee as incense; and the lifting up of my hands as the evening sacrifice." See also Genesis 8:21, where God smells the savour of Noah's sacrifice after the Flood and decides not to destroy the world again.

p. 17, *Louis the Just*: A sobriquet of Louis XIII, who reigned from 1610 to 1643.

p. 17, *Achab*: Achab seems to be an invented figure: there is no mention in the Bible of Noah having any daughters, and in any case, "Achab" (French for "Ahab", as in the king of Israel) is a masculine name.

p. 20, *chariot of fire*: Elijah did indeed rise to heaven in a chariot: see 2 Kings 2:11.

p. 22, *Aesculapius... of their hosts*: Aesculapius was the Greek god of medicine, and he is regularly associated with snakes; Scipio was the name of two famous Roman generals; Alexander is "the Great"; Charles Martel (early eighth century) was a Frankish military leader; Edward could be one of several kings of England. Snakes do seem to have played a part in the posthumous existence of some of the men mentioned here: for example, when the tomb of Charles Martel was opened some years after his death, his body had apparently been replaced by a great snake (or, on other accounts, a black dragon).

p. 22, *And to show... its head*: See Genesis 3:15, where God tells the serpent after the Fall· "And I will put enmity between thee and the woman, and between thy seed and her seed; it shall bruise thy head, and thou shalt bruise his heel."

p. 25, *the eleven thousand virgins*: The eleven thousand virgins associated with St Ursula were massacred by the Huns near Cologne.

p. 25, *Our Lady's cotton*: The floating, feathery seed from the milk thistle or St Mary's thistle.

p. 25, *assumptions... the Evangelist*: St John was taken up into heaven when he had the vision detailed in the Book of Revelation.

p. 29, *Socrates' demon*: That is, his *daimon*, or familiar spirit, which, according to Plato's *Apology*, only warned Socrates what *not* to do, and never gave positive advice.

p. 29, *Epaminondas... Brutus*: Epaminondas (d. 362 BC) was a Theban statesman much admired in the Renaissance (especially by Montaigne) for his probity. Cato the Younger (d. 46 BC) was a Stoic and an opponent of Julius Caesar; Brutus (d. 42 BC), a relative of Cato's, was one of Caesar's assassins.

p. 29, *Drusus... go any further*: Drusus (full name Nero Claudius Drusus Germanicus, 38 BC–9 BC) was the son of Livia Drusilla and the stepson (or, as was commonly thought, son) of the Emperor Augustus (Livia married Augustus shortly after her divorce from her first husband). Drusus waged war in Germany; while campaigning near the Elbe he is said to have seen the shape of a Germanic woman warning him to turn back. He did so, but died soon afterwards after falling from his horse.

p. 29, *Agrippa... magicians*: Agrippa von Nettesheim (d. 1535) was accused of black magic; the "Abbé Tritème", better known as Johannes Trithemius (d. 1516; his birth name was Johann Heidenberg, and his assumed surname Trithemius means "from Trittenheim", his birthplace on the Moselle) was an alchemist who corresponded with Agrippa; Johan Faustus (d. *c.*1540), the basis for later Fausts, was a real character who knew Agrippa and Johannes; Guy de La Brosse (d. 1641) was a botanist and the personal physician of Louis XIII; "César" is unclear – possibly Cesare Ripa (d. *c.* 622), an Italian who wrote a famous book on emblems and their allegorical significance, the *Iconologia*. The "Knights of the Rosy Cross" are the Rosicrucians.

p. 29, *Campanella*: Tommaso Campanella (d. 1639), author of the utopian *The City of the Sun*, was tried for heresy.

p. 30, *De sensu rerum*: *De sensu rerum et magia*, or *On the Meaning of Things and on Magic*, a work by Campanella (1620). See previous note.

p. 30, *La Mothe Le Vayer and Gassendi*: François de La Mothe Le Vayer (d. 1672) was a rationalist of sceptical bent; he tutored Louis XIV and was a friend of Molière. For Gassendi, see note to p. 7.

p. 30, *Tristan L'Hermite*: Born François L'Hermite, Tristan L'Hermite (d. 1655) was a poet, playwright and personal friend of Cyrano; he had to flee from France (initially to Britain) after killing his opponent in a duel, aged only thirteen.

p. 30, *talcum... eternity*: These terms are all derived from alchemy.

p. 30, *disdain... in his barrel*: Diogenes the Cynic (d. 327 BC) lived in a tub and led a life marked by his contempt for conventions. Alexander the Great visited him and asked if he could do anything for him. Diogenes replied, "Stand a little out of the sunlight."

p. 39, *sixain*: A sixain is a stanza of six lines.

p. 39, *Sorel... clearly*: Charles Sorel (d. 1672) wrote the first French picaresque novel *La vraie histoire comique de Francion* (1622). Hortensius is a writer in this novel.

p. 40, *criado de nuestra mercede*: "I am Our Grace's humble servant" (formal Spanish).

p. 41, *unless you wear... surplice*: In other words, unless you are an academic, physician or priest.

p. 42, *antiperistasis*: A term in ancient Greek physics used to refer to the way a body reacts to its surroundings.

p. 44, *the Gordian knot... Alexander*: A legend in which Alexander the Great cut through an intricate knot, the untier of which was prophesied to become the ruler of Asia.

p. 45, *I think... open our stomachs*: Cyrano's at times baroque physics can indeed be difficult to follow, however intellectually appetizing it may be. As Madeleine Alcover suggests, the terms he uses reflect the intellectual turmoil of an age struggling to free itself from Aristotle and develop a new, post-Galilean world view.

p. 47, *Peripatetics*: The followers of Aristotle.

p. 61, *Hercules... reached forty*: Not true: Julius Caesar (100–44 BC) was fifty-five when he was assassinated.

p. 63, *Caesar was... upon him*: Cassius was one of the conspirators against Caesar, and, in the civil wars that followed, lost to Mark Antony, whereupon he asked his freedman Pindarus to slay him.

p. 64, *under a gooseberry bush*: The French has "under a head of cabbage".

p. 66, *Diogenes... sighs for Lais*: The courtesan Lais of Corinth is usually associated with the philosopher Aristippus (who wrote of her charms) rather than with Diogenes (see fifth note to p. 30).

p. 73, *miteyness*: "Miteyness" is a neologism based on Cyrano's own *cironalité* ("*ciron*" means "mite").

p. 83, *steel square*: The tip of a crossbow projectile.

p. 84, *The States and Empires of the Sun*: Cyrano's companion piece to the present work.

p. 84, *The Great Work of the Philosophers*: This reference is unclear, though it may be to a sixteenth-century work on alchemy by Rouillac Piémontois; *great work* was a term commonly used in alchemy.

p. 90, *the part of shame*: Pudendum, "that of which one ought to be ashamed" (Latin).

p. 91, *obliged to give a pistole... yesterday*: A pistole and an *écu* were coins, the former and more valuable of the two being a gold coin, often Spanish in origin.

p. 96, *Quinze-Vingts hospice*: The Hôpital des Quinze-Vingts was a hospital for the blind.

p. 98, *For if... no better off than us*: This argument has some similarity to Pascal's Wager.

p. 98, *play hide and seek with men*: Pascal, among others, pondered on God's self-concealment – the theme of the "*Dieu caché*" or "hidden God".

MORE 101-PAGE CLASSICS

FOR THE FULL LIST OF
101-PAGE CLASSICS VISIT
101pages.co.uk

ALMA CLASSICS

ALMA CLASSICS aims to publish mainstream and lesser-known European classics in an innovative and striking way, while employing the highest editorial and production standards. By way of a unique approach the range offers much more, both visually and textually, than readers have come to expect from contemporary classics publishing.

LATEST TITLES PUBLISHED BY ALMA CLASSICS

www.almaclassics.com